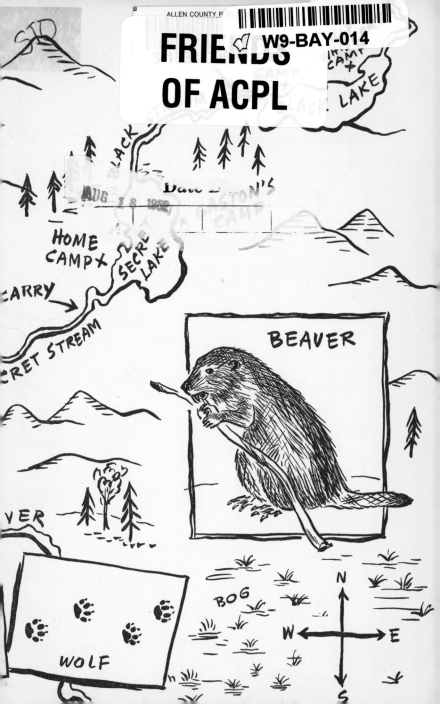

By Lew Dietz

JEFF WHITE: YOUNG WOODSMAN
JEFF WHITE: YOUNG TRAPPER

JEFF WHITE:
Young Trapper

Line drawings by William Moyers

JEFF WHITE:
Young Trapper

by

Lew Dietz

Boston

Little, Brown and Company · 1951

FIRST EDITION

Published February 1951

*Published simultaneously
in Canada by McClelland and Stewart Limited*

PRINTED IN THE UNITED STATES OF AMERICA

To the men of Maine's Department of Inland Fisheries and Game who, performing yeoman service, have helped to preserve Jeff White's wilderness, this book is warmly dedicated.

Contents

CONTENTS

JEFF WHITE:
Young Trapper

1. A Dead Moose

THE KEENING WIND hunting down off the mountain had a bite in it. Jeff White turned up his shirt collar, yanked his gunning cap down over his ears and shouldered his ax. Pappy Newlin had taken the load of fir boughs out the tote road with the team, and the tinkling harness bells, distancing now, sounded strangely unreal in the owl-light of the northern dusk.

It recalled to Jeff, as he strode out across the meadow towards the low-lying farmhouse, a city sound he had heard as a boy. There had been an old bearded junkman who drove an ancient horse along the cobbled streets. He had a bell like that and he would plead in a sad singsong voice for old rags and paper. It seemed so long ago and yet it was barely a year and a half since he had come from the city to live in this wilderness country.

He walked toward the beckoning light of the farm, his young, seasoned body comfortably tired from the afternoon chore. Ma had needed some more fir boughs for winter banking around the house foundation. It was good

3

work, for he liked the feel of an ax in his hands; he liked the sound of the blade cutting deep and the sight of yellow chips flying.

He felt at home in the woods. Perhaps this was strange, for, although he had been born in this Deep River Country, he had been taken to live in the city with relatives as a small child, and the city had been his home through most of his growing years.

On the other hand, perhaps it would have been more strange if the woods had seemed foreign and forbidding, for his father, Luke White, had been a famous woodsman. There was a quartering of Indian blood in his father's veins and the tribal blood was in him, too. It would have been even more strange, considering his heritage, if coming back had not seemed like coming home.

Pappy had reached the road and Jeff heard his voice as he geed the horses on the homeward stretch. The prospect of food was just about the only thing that could hurry Pappy. Eating was the one job that the Hibbses' hired hand tackled with gusto. It was old Gramp's public opinion that Pappy ate more than he was worth and, although Jeff never took sides in their eternal arguments, he was inclined to agree that it would take a good man to be worth what Pappy Newlin consumed in the way of vittles.

But Pappy had been a fixture in the household for years,

4

and Jeff was certain that his absence would be missed and that no one would miss him more than Gramp himself.

"It's bad enough," Ma had once said, "to have those two going at it tooth and nail. But I'd hate to see what it would be like around here if Gramp didn't have anyone to bounce his orneriness against. If Gramp didn't have Pappy around, he'd be too cussed to live with."

So, all in all, it was a fine and happy household that Jeff White had become a part of. Will Hibbs, warden of the State Inland Fish and Game Department, had become, in the brief months since his arrival, more than a father to him. He was a warm friend and companion. And Ma Hibbs, Will's plump, competent wife, couldn't have been more kind if he had been her own son. To Jeff she was Ma as she was to all the countryside. And as for Will Hibbs, he had become, after a few weeks of Mr. Hibbs and then Uncle Will, just plain Will.

Pappy was already in the kitchen, his long, thin nose sniffing the frying venison when Jeff stepped in from the shed. He saw that Will hadn't yet come home, for his blue warden's jacket and cap weren't hanging from their customary peg.

"Will's late," Jeff said.

Ma was jostling the sizzling venison in the pan with a fork. "I expect Will when I see him. You ought to know

5

that by now, Jeff. You get washed up and set. You think you could eat, boys?"

"Fried venison!" Pappy whispered almost reverently. "That's just the proper dish for a couple of hard workin' wood choppers!" Pappy was tall and thin as a split rail and there was a hound-dog sadness in his eyes. This generally lugubrious air was countered by his large, humorous mouth, habitually twirked at its corners by inward amusement.

"Ma," Pappy avowed, "Jefferson and me have done a considerable job of work today. I am of the opinion we should have a little extra portion of that delectable steak."

"If I know you, Pappy Newlin," Ma said, "it was Jeff who did most of the work. Just call Gramp in and set down. You'll get fed."

"What's 'at! What's that worm-eaten splinter sayin' 'bout me now?" Old Gramp's bent figure hove into the doorway, his fierce little eyes turned upon Pappy.

"Sit down, Gramp," Ma said mildly; "it's time to eat."

"That's what I thought he said and it's a crawlin' lie! Deer meat oughter be cooked rare — blood red. Just kiss the skillet and flip her over. Good thing I happened in or that drink a water would have had it all et up and lickin' at the platter like a hound dog."

"Happy little fella, ain't he now," Pappy ventured benignly. "Blessed with one of them sweet dispositions,

6

Gramp is. Too bad he's deaf as a dogfish and hasn't got a tooth in his head. Now don't go too easy on them mashed potatoes, Ma."

Gramp's eyes were now diverted by the heaping plates that Ma was placing on the checkered tablecloth. Though Gramp had, in fact, only one good ear and even the good one wasn't very reliable, his eyes and his nose were unimpaired. And despite his rheumatic limbs, he could spot Pappy ten feet and usually beat him to the supper table. He did just that.

"May be run-out and too old to keep up with the best of 'em in the woods, but I can still eat!" Gramp muttered with deep satisfaction. "Red meat, there's the stuff to lard a man's ribs! Go to it, boy."

The three went to it without further ado. Ma stood by at the stove watching the food disappear, for it was her habit to wait for her warden husband when Will was late.

She looked up expectantly now, for a car had come into the yard. But this wasn't Will's car. His car was full of rattles and this one had come up like a purring cat. There were booted steps on the stoop. Ma moved across the kitchen and opened the door to reveal a stalwart figure in the powder-blue uniform of the State Police. Jeff recognized the rubicund face of Trooper Jack Bailey.

Concern must have shown on Ma's face, for Jack boomed quickly: "Nothing serious, Ma. A car hit a moose, that's all. I was on my way back to the barracks for supper and met Will on the River Road. Will is apt to be late, for a moose is a large animal."

"And you," Ma retorted with asperity, "are a big cop. I'd like to bet you moseyed right along to get *your* supper."

Jack stepped in and his big square body seemed to fill the kitchen. He nodded to Gramp and Pappy and winked broadly at Jeff.

"How many times has Will said that a state cop is no earthly good ten yards off a highway? That moose was ten yards out of bounds for me. Will asked me to call you, but big-hearted me, I stopped by. Hmmm, venison. There's some compensation for being a warden, at that."

"Yes, that's venison," Ma said. "And we come by it the same way you might if you knew how to handle a rifle and didn't get lost in a wood lot. You leave Will dressing out a moose on a back road and now you want to eat his supper."

Jack loosened his tunic, let out his belt and hooked a chair under him with a booted foot. "I'll tell you what I'll do, Ma," Jack said, "I'll be fair. I'll divide it with him."

Ma looked ceilingward in mock resignation. "Get a plate, Jack. How long's Will apt to be? He'll have to load that moose and get it to the hospital or some institution tonight."

8

"That's right, the meat goes to charity, doesn't it? Yes, this would be a good week for me to have an operation. They'll be serving moose meat at the county hospital. Will won't be too long. I sent a wrecker back to help the car out of the ditch. They'll give him a hand."

The heaping plate was set down before him. Jack massaged his hands. "Get ready, stomach, here it comes! Nothing like an accident to give a man an appetite."

"That car must have been smashed up pretty bad," Jeff suggested.

Jack was already forking up the food. "Not too bad, considering. His radiator grille and fenders will never be the same, but the car, once he gets it back on the road, ought to percolate. Fellow by the name of Quigley driving the car. Talkative fellow, needed a shave. He's on his way into the Black Lakes for some late hunting. *Too* late for my taste. Hate to be caught in there in a snowstorm."

Pappy and Gramp were finishing in a dead heat when they heard Will Hibbs's car rattle into the yard. A moment later the door swung back to admit the warden's tall figure.

"I'll bet," Ma greeted him slyly, "you're hungry enough to eat a moose, Will."

"Not a moose but I could eat a big cop, buttons and all," Will replied grimly. He was looking darkly at Jack. "A fine mess you left me with. That fellow Dobson had a

9

loaded rifle in the back seat. He was just a bit on the nasty side when I handed him an invitation to appear in court. Don't you know it's a violation of the game laws to carry a loaded gun in your car, Jack?"

"Now, Will," Jack said placidly as he mopped up his plate, "is it a cop's job to check hunting rifles?" Jack had been chewing. All at once he stopped chewing. "Dobson? I checked his driver's license. His name is Quigley."

Will tossed his hat on the peg and bent over the sink to clean up. "I checked his hunting license. His name is Harry Dobson. He's six feet tall, forty years old. And I don't mind telling you I don't like him."

"Harry Dobson!" Jack sat bolt upright. "Look Will, cover me on this! I helped him out of a ditch. Where's your phone?"

"What's wrong with a cop helping a man out of a ditch?"

"Nothing much," Jack barked, "ordinarily. But this one happens to be wanted for a little matter of stealing a fifty-thousand-dollar lumber company payroll!"

All eyes turned to the trooper as he shouted to the operator: "State Police. Get me through fast to Bingham Barracks . . . !"

Will's large mouth was working up a slow grin. "Bring it on. I think I'm sure going to enjoy my supper tonight. Jack, I'm taking a day off tomorrow. Jeff and the sheriff and I are going rabbit hunting. If you're not going to be busy, maybe you'd like to come along."

At the phone, Jack's face was flushed with discomfort. "Comedian!" Jack snorted. And then — "Pete? Jack. Get this out to all patrols, Deer River and north. . . ."

2. The Strange Case of Willy Whiskers

JEFF WHITE, shotgun under the crook of his arm, stood by the river, one booted foot on the trunk of a blowdown. The fallen giant, rotting and moss-coated, lay half in the stream, and the sluggish current eddied around its dark, drowned branches.

Thoughtfully, absently, Jeff poked at the decaying ancient with his toe. What had once been a towering spruce, its spire thrust skyward, was now more a part of the earth than the sky. The great root ball, uptorn by some forgotten wind, would have filled a room.

"Fifty years ago, maybe," Jeff thought, "it came down with a crash."

And his dark eyes reached up the river wondering then, as he had often wondered of late, how this all had looked to those first, seeking eyes — to those who had come before the roads, before the maps, compelled by a nagging urge to explore the unknown.

It was a golden day in late October, and the sun lay like

a benediction over the wooded land — an Indian summer day that seemed to smile and say, "Don't be taken in, this can't last."

He was just thinking about how soon the cold would come. The squirrels were not fooled. They were busy storing acorns. The bears were gourmandizing with beechnuts and berries, putting on their winter coat of fat that was to sustain them through the barren months ahead. What was he doing? Winter would come upon him, perhaps overnight. He had to make plans too. He had to be ready.

Jeff stood there, reposefully, gazing north — upstream towards the distant headwaters of the Deer River. Thirty miles to the northward, Deer River fed out of Squaw Lake. Beyond Squaw Lake was Secret and then Black Lake. Beyond Black Lake were more streams, with innumerable falls and roaring rapids, appearing on the maps like the threads upon which the many lakes of the lake country were strung like pearls. Shelter Lake — Fisher Lake — Hatchet Lake — Dead Man's Pond.

For more than a year now he had lived on the threshold of the wilderness. To the north lay the wild lands. To the north lay a country of unorganized townships designated only by numbers and letters. Into that wild, inaccessible country, logging operations had come and gone and would come again, yet there still remained some tracts of virgin timber standing as it had stood for centuries. Lumbering had changed the geography here and there. Some land had been drowned to make a head of water for log drives. Yet, all in all, Jeff was sure, the country hadn't changed too much since the first white man beheld it.

No, it couldn't have changed too much since that unremembered moment when a tiny dot had appeared on the slow moving river. Finally, you could see the shape of it and the glint of the sun on whipping paddles. In the bow stood a white man, his eyes hollowed by fatigue, his skin streaked with the blood of myriads of biting insects. Carrying him forward were the paddles plied by coppery arms. The eagle feathers bobbed in unison with each rhythmic stroke. The white man's boat swept on northward and was gone again into the unknown.

Beaver had been the lure to open a new continent. Beaver! The magic word that had made empires. Long before the first white man's bateau had been poled up the river, the Indian had prized the beaver. The fur of the beaver was warm and snug. It was soft as a baby's skin, yet the keenest blade was needed to mar it. Long before the first French *voyageur* had explored the rivers of the new world, the beaver pelt was the standard of value in barter among the tribes. The white man came seeking gold. This satiny pelt of the wilderness engineer was the gold they found. The ships returned home, beaver skins in their holds. This cargo was gold, for this was the stuff that kings' hats were made of in those days when kings ruled with a wave of a hand.

All this Jeff White knew from the books he had read. Jeff smiled a little at his fantasy. Yet it wasn't entirely a fantasy, for that river still led into beaver country and the lure was still there. What was there about lonely country that called a fellow? He didn't know exactly. All Jeff could say was that he had the itch to spend a winter in that Black Lake Country. It was a challenge, maybe that was it. Whatever it was, it had him right by the scruff of the neck. He wanted to "go in," as the local phrase put it. It didn't make much sense, this crazy urge, when you looked it right in the face. But others had felt it before. . . .

Warden Will Hibbs stepped out of the thicket to the bank of the river. Glancing downstream he saw the boy standing there, deep in reflection. He studied the boy, idly, struck again by his resemblance to his famous and well-remembered father, Luke. He had noted the likeness when he first had laid eyes on the boy. Now the months in the woods had seasoned him, leaned out the boyish contours of his face. Seeing him now, standing motionless against the backdrop of the woods, Will

15

was startled as though come upon a ghost from the past.

"The very spit'n image," Will said aloud.

Will moved to dig for his pipe and the motion caught the boy's eye. The boy grinned and waved his hand. "Where's the sheriff gone with those dogs?" he called.

"Heard them running over back of Burnt Hill a while back," Will said. "They were running wild. Must have got into one of those racers. Shall we work back towards the road?"

Jeff fanned out his hand in agreement. As he joined the warden, he caught the sound of the running dogs. They were far off, tonguing in wild excitement, moving to the westward.

"They're going good," Jeff said appreciatively. "Are you sure that's a rabbit they're running?"

"They may be on a fox," Will said. "Parker insists those hounds of his are well-trained and won't touch a fox scent, but I've never seen a rabbit hound yet that won't get tempted by a fox track now and then. A fox leaves a strong and mighty exciting scent. Most likely, though, that pair have got onto one of those racers."

Jeff nodded. He'd heard the boys speak of those deep-woods rabbits that run wild and wide and were as apt as not to take a dog over a couple of mountains instead of sticking, like a reasonable hare, in a single wood patch.

They were in a piece of low-lying thicket between the

river and the Deer River Road. Together they pushed towards the road through a growth of alder and birch. Halfway out, Jeff retrieved a brace of rabbits he'd shot earlier that day. They were varying hares. Snowshoe rabbits, they were called locally. Their coats were already turning from brown to winter white.

Jeff slung them over his shoulder. Will smiled. "If you've never had one of Ma's rabbit stews, you've got a treat in store for you, Tracker."

"I've never had anything that Ma's cooked that wasn't a treat," Jeff said. "Hey — here they come! They're driving this way, fast!"

They were heading their way all right, tonguing steady and right on the line. Jeff dropped his rabbits and fanned out away from Will to find a stand.

"This may save me from a skunk," Will said. "I haven't had a good shot all day."

Jeff had moved barely twenty yards when he saw Will's gun go to his shoulder. The big twelve-gauge slammed once. Twice. Then Jeff saw a bounding ghost streaking on its way to disappear into the alders.

"You missed him," Jeff called. "Too bad."

"That's the fastest doggone bunny I ever did see!" Will muttered. "Missed him clean."

The pursuing hounds whirled into view, running fast, their brittle voices raised in high exaltation. They were gone again in a glimmering. It was just then that another gun spoke to the right. There was only one report this time. In a moment they heard the sound of the dogs at the kill and Parker West's voice drawling his approval.

Will appeared chagrined. "That's Park's third. You've got two. I guess this just isn't my day." He cupped his hands over his mouth and yelled to the sheriff. "We're headed out, Parker. See you on the road."

"Need any help toting your rabbits out," Parker shouted back. "What were you shootin' at just then?"

"Signal shot," Will called back. "I thought maybe those hounds of yours had got you lost."

Will was ahead as they broke out on the road. Jeff saw him stop suddenly, his eyes fixed on something up the road. Jeff emerged just in time to see a queer, unshaven figure in a long black coat disappear into the thicket across the road. Behind the furtive figure trailed a large dog.

"What the dickens was that?" Jeff asked in astonishment.

"Willy Whiskers," Will said thoughtfully. "He's a long way from home."

"Willy Whiskers?"

"That's what he's called. No one knows his real name or anything about him. Fifteen years ago he suddenly appeared in Boulder, bought some supplies and a canoe and headed in. He's got a cabin on Black Lake. Willy and that Malemute dog of his are inseparable. He's never come out again. Buck Larrabee runs into him now and then. That's Buck's district."

At that moment Parker West came out on the road, the leash of the tugging dogs grasped in his hand. He was a small, wiry man in a stained felt hat. His pants, some three inches too large at the waist, were held up by a pair of brilliant red suspenders.

Will said: "Just saw Willy Whiskers ducking into the brush. Has he moved back here into your county, Park?"

"Willy?" He looked interested. "Not that I know of. Maybe he's come down to see Old Carrie. Willy's shy as a fox and she's the only one he'll have any dealings with in these parts. She gets supplies for him, such as they are. They tell me all he needs to survive is a box of salt. Glad to hear Willy's still alive and kicking."

"Did you have any reason to think he wasn't?" Will asked.

"Nope. Only I had a call some weeks back. A man wanted to know about Willy. Wanted to know if he was still around. Said he was a friend of his and was interested."

Will was down on the grass patting the tired hounds. Will smiled. "You know what Buck has to do every year? He knows Willy won't come in and buy a license.

He also knows he'd never get him into court if he summoned him. So each year he delivers Will's license to him. He cruises in and slips it under his camp door. And Willy slips the money out through a crack. He's got some of those oversized bills that have been out of circulation for years."

Parker shook his head. "There are some queer stories about Willy. Some say he's well educated. Some say he's got a sockful of money. If he's got money, he sure hasn't anything to spend it on out in that Lake Country. Must be some kind of a nut, that Willy."

Jeff broke his gun. The shells slid out into the palm of his hand. "Does a fellow," he said musingly, "need to be some kind of nut to enjoy a winter in that Black Lake Country? It doesn't sound so bad."

Both men turned to the boy. Again Will Hibbs was struck by this strange glint in his quiet eyes. "Just what have you got on your mind, Tracker?" Will drawled.

Jeff dropped the shells into his pocket and shrugged. "I guess I was just thinking out loud. Don't the wardens have a camp in there on Secret Lake? I thought I heard Warden Larrabee say he was going to cruise in there and provision it before the ice seals up the lakes."

"What big ears you have, Tracker," Will said with a smile. "And you want to hook up with him, is that it?"

Sheriff West looked up with sharp interest. "Say now,

if Buck's going in, he might look out for that Dobson feller. The state cops never did find that character. A canoe was stole from a fishing camp on Little Dog Stream. Kinder figure myself he went into that country to rusticate. Hate to have to go there myself with the dogs running so good. Chances are he's gone clear out of my county anyway."

Will shook his head. "You talk as though the wardens haven't been doing all your woods work for years so you can go rabbit hunting. If Buck sees this fellow, he'll tell him you're looking for him. Well, let's stir our stumps."

"But I would like to go in with Buck," Jeff pressed him. "You see it's my chance to get my own provisions in before the ice."

Will's head came up. "Huh! What's this? You may be a born woodsman, Tracker, but you're not a winter woodsman yet. Just what have you got on your mind?"

"Fur," Jeff said softly. "If I can get Sampson to stake me, I'd like to try trapping this winter."

"Holy ole mackinaw!" Will exclaimed. "When did you stumble on that wild notion?"

"The fact is," Jeff said, "just about two minutes ago."

3. Jeff Makes a Deal

THE HIBBS FARM stands ten miles north of the small village of Boulder on Route 6 or, as it was locally called, the Border Road. The highway is promising enough as you leave the village, winding sleek and black across wooded terrain, spanning culverted streams that run swift and white over glacial rocks towards the peaceful valley land to the south.

Six miles north of Boulder, Route 6 degenerates into a gravel road kept dragged and smooth in the summer but nigh impassable in the mud season when the frost is working out of the earth. In the winter, it's sometimes as long as a week after a heavy snowfall before the state plow bucks its way north through the drifts to free the few, lonely farm dwellers out Warden Hibbs's way.

The plow seldom bothers to clear much beyond the Hibbs farm, for there is nothing much beyond there but wilderness — one hundred miles of it — until you come upon the border town of Barter. Once the Border Road had been a stage turnpike, but today the main communications to Canada all lay to the eastward. Twenty miles above the Hibbs farm all there is to beckon travelers on is a set of rutted wagon tracks that seem to get more and more discouraged as they wend northward. Soon all that remains is a wilderness logging trail cutting through unending ranks of lancing spruce.

And it is twenty miles above the Hibbs farm that the road veers west and the river turns east. A traveler has his choice, of course. The river is a highway, too, the only avenue into one of the few remaining stretches of wild land still untapped by man-made arteries. This is the Black Lake District.

This was the highway that Jeff White saw in his mind's eye that night as he sat in the barn in the yellow light of a kerosene lamp and finished dressing his rabbits. He hung them in the fur over a rafter and, cleaning his hunting knife, sat down on the chopping block to whetstone its edge.

Beyond in the house, the supper bustle was over and evening quiet had come. Warden Hibbs and Ma were seated in the kitchen preparing a winter provision list for Pappy Newlin to fetch in from the village the next day. Pappy, his voracious appetite reasonably satisfied, had gone to his room with a dog-eared Western pulp magazine. Old Gramp, finding no listeners for his colored tales of youthful prowess and no target for his smoldering wrath, had set his bent frame into the easy chair in the living room to go through a two-foot stack of trapping and hunting catalogues he had accumulated over the years and guarded jealously.

At least, that was where Jeff had left the old man. He turned now at the sound of a creaking door. Gramp's seamed face peered in at him.

"What yer doin' out here, boy?"

"Just dressing those rabbits, Gramp. Come on in."

"Hmmm," Gramp muttered, "rabbits! How I uster hate them rabbits. Gad blamed nuisance, that's what they were!"

"Don't you like rabbit stew?"

Gramp hobbled on in and set himself down beside Jeff on the chopping block. "Why when I was just a nipper, they was so thick a man agoin' through the woods would trip over the cussed things. A man, he'd set his traps, spend all day makin' sets and come back to tend 'em and what would he find? Rabbits! I've et biled rabbits, fried rabbits, pickled rabbits until they come out my ears. A man can get a bellyful of rabbits."

Jeff looked down, narrowly, at the old man. "You've heard about my plans, Gramp. You used to trap. What do you think?"

"Trap! Why when I was hardly ten years old, I run a

trap line in a hundred-and-fifty-mile circle up in that country."

"Ten years old!"

"Well, mebbe fifteen, it was. What's the difference of five years when a man's my age. Uster be plenty a fine beaver, fisher and marten in them days. And mind yer, we had some real winters back a way. Ten feet a snow, fifty below! Why, if a man stepped out of his snowshoes, he'd just go clean out a sight and that's a fact."

"Must have been pretty rugged," Jeff agreed. "What made the snow so deep in those days?"

"What made it! How should I know! Everythin's changed and that's a fact. Why, back in them days, we used to have wolves huntin' in packs, keepin' everythin' on the jump. And them pesky wolverines. Why one a them rascally beggers would foller a trapper all day long an' steal the bait out of his trap just as fast as he'd bait 'em. Things have changed." Gramp shook his old head sadly. "Yes sir, it ain't what it uster be."

"But I guess," Jeff said, "it still isn't any picnic. Just last winter a couple of trappers went in and never came out."

"Greenhorns!" Gramp snorted.

Jeff smiled. "What about me, Gramp? I'm still kind of a greenhorn."

"You!" Gramp was indignant. "You ain't no greenhorn, boy! I knew by the cut of yer the first time I set eyes on

25

yer. 'That's Luke White's boy,' I sez to myself 'There's a born woodsman and no mistake.' "

"Then maybe," Jeff said carefully, "you'd mention that to Ma. The fact is she's trying to talk me out of this crazy notion, as she calls it."

Gramp slapped his bony knee. "Wimmin! Don't you pay no heed to wimmin's talk, boy. You head in. You'll make out. Why, if I was just ten years younger, I'd head in with yer, that's a fact."

"But I still have to get my stake. I won't let Will back me. I've got to do this on my own. If the Sampson Fur Company will back me, I'll know it's because they feel I can produce some fur. It'll be a business proposition."

"You just go see old Andy. Just tell him I sent yer, boy."

"Andy Sampson? He's dead, Gramp," Jeff pointed out mildly. "They tell me he's been dead twenty years. It's his son Ernie who runs the place now."

"So he is. So he is." Gramp shook his old head bitterly. "Why is it the old-timers all got ter die off? No more old-timers left. Not a real wilderness trapper left. Airplane trappers! Air pirates, I calls 'em! Hop in an' hop out. Uster take Joe LeBlanc an' me six days to get to our territory. Fishers was our meat in them days. A good fisher fetched a hundred fifty dollars. Why one time I mind me an' Joe tracked a fisher for three days afore he holed inter a holler log."

"Did you know where you were after all that time? Haven't you ever been lost, Gramp?"

Gramp snorted. "Lost? Kinder depends how a man looks at it now. I mind the time Joe didn't turn up for two weeks an' I got kinder troubled. A couple of Frenchmen were tryin' to get into our territory an' I was thinkin' maybe Joe had run afoul a them poachers. But then one day along comes Joe. He comes in and brews hisself a cup a tea. Finally I says, 'Joe, you been lost?' 'Lost!' Joe says. 'Can't say as I was lost. I was jist kind a bewildered for a week, ten days.'"

"Did you ever get those fellows who were trying to get your territory?" Jeff asked.

Gramp chuckled. "They met up with Joe one day on Little Black Stream and cut his throat from ear to ear when he wasn't lookin'. They slit him up and left Joe fer dead. Three weeks later, they were at the stopover at Bright Lake Farm on the way out and Joe walks up to them, big as life. Joe says 'Boys, the only way you can kill Joe LeBlanc is to take his head an' hide it.' An' then Joe takes out his knife and carves up them fellers so bad it took three docs to get 'em whole again. There was a tough ol' wilderness trapper. Joe'll be dead twenty year now, God rest his ugly soul."

"Do you think Ernie will back me? I'm going to see him tomorrow."

"You jus' let me know if he don't!" Gramp snorted. "I'll give him a piece a my mind. I may look run-out but I still got plenty a vinegar in me yet. You just let me know, boy."

Ma and Will Hibbs were still bent over the kitchen table, checking their list, when Jeff came in from the shed.

Ma looked up and sighed in resignation. "I guess there's not a mite of sense in my being grim about this thing, Jeff. You men! It does seem to me that just keeping warm and well fed is enough of a struggle in the winter, without going out asking for trouble."

Will caught Jeff's eyes and winked broadly. "Men are just simple critters, Ma. You just don't know what it's like to be out on snowshoes fifty miles from a living soul, after a fresh fall of snow."

"I most certainly don't!" Ma agreed, warmly. "And I most certainly never plan to find out." But her eyes were soft as they sought Jeff's face. "All I can say is that there's no accounting for tastes. Well, go to it, Jeff, with my blessings. And take care of yourself."

Ma turned back quickly to her list. "Two hundred of flour and fifty of sugar ought to do us, Will."

"I'll take care of myself, Ma." Jeff said quietly.

There was rain in the wind and great black, scudding

clouds were sweeping across the sky as Jeff and Pappy prepared to depart for the village the next morning.

Pappy had gone back into the barn for the five-gallon kerosene can. Jeff was climbing aboard the pickup truck when he heard the faint sound in the heavens. He lifted his head and it came again, thin and clear now. Then he saw the flight of dark wedges scraping the treetops — Canada geese cutting their way southward.

Jeff knew what this meant. This meant the end of open water. Perhaps the freeze wouldn't come at once but it would come soon. From now on every day counted. The sense of urgency ran swiftly through him. He had to convince Ernie Sampson. He had to get his stake and be on his way.

The Sampson Fur Company was housed in what had once been a large barn. It stood behind a low, white house on the edge of the village, proclaimed by a sign featuring what looked like a bear, although Ernie insisted it was meant to be a fox.

When Jeff stepped into the store that morning, Ernie was talking to Gaston LaFleur, one of the region's most storied trappers. Gaston, stocky and bull-voiced, had come down from French Canada some years before, and the extravagant tales he'd brought with him of his life in the Canadian wilderness, even when cut down to size as they were by his listeners, were blood-tingling. Gaston

29

was blessed with a high sense of the dramatic and he dressed in keeping with his talents. He wore an otter hat and a large blanket-thick mackinaw with wide horizontal stripes.

Seeing Jeff, Gaston offered a white grin. "'Allo, Jeff! How's the boy, yes? You catch nuther bearskin, may be?"

Ernie Sampson nodded genially. "You look like you have something on your mind, Jeff. You don't figure to try your hand at trapping this winter, do you?"

"Fact is," Jeff said, taking advantage of the opening, "that's just what I have got in mind. How's the trapping going to be this year, Gaston?"

"Oooh, plenty fur, plenty fur," Gaston said with an easy gesture. "I cruise in by Swan Lake las' week. Plenty rabbits. Plenty rabbits, plenty fur."

This was his opening! What if Ernie laughed at him? After all, Ernie was a businessman and he was a greenhorn. Jeff moistened his lips, his eyes running over the cluttered store, heaped with traps and guns and woodsman's supplies.

Jeff swallowed. "How much," he began cautiously, "would it take to set a fellow up with fifty traps and grub this winter?"

Ernie studied the boy carefully. "That kind of all depends, Jeff, on how big a piece a man wants to tackle and how long he plans to stay in. What about it, Gaston?"

Gaston looked at Jeff, impressed. "You go in for fur this winter, Jeff?"

Jeff nodded. "Yes, I am, if I can get Mr. Sampson to stake me."

Gaston's eyes popped. Suddenly a roar of laughter exploded from him. He slapped his thighs. "So? Thees a man right from my heart! Right from the shoulder, hey. Thees kind a fella get plenty fur, Ernie."

Ernie appeared a little uncomfortable. He sat his bulk on the edge of the counter. He took out his pipe and examined it carefully. "Trapping, young feller, is a very hazardous and speculative occupation."

Gaston nodded eloquently, feeling his ears. "She col' like blazes! Frostbite, may be. Lose ears. Lose feet. Lose everythings!"

Jeff took a deep, sustaining breath. "I don't want you to back me unless you think I can produce, Mr. Sampson, unless you think I'm a good investment. You're a businessman."

Gaston slapped his thighs again in huge enjoyment. "I like thees. Businessman? Ernie, he's a robber! For ten fox in fine fur, he tell Gaston twelve dollair!"

Ernie tolerantly ignored Gaston's reflections on his integrity. "Where do you plan to work, Jeff? Mind you," he warned, "I'm not committing myself."

Jeff had his map out. He spread it flat on the counter.

31

Both Ernie and Gaston bent over his shoulder. As his finger traced a line up along the upper reaches of Deer River and into the Black Lake Country, he explained:

"Warden Larrabee cruised out that country with the warden pilot. He tells me there are plenty of live beaver flowages in there and he thinks there's a good chance it will be opened for beaver trapping this winter. We won't know until after the reports go into Augusta to the commissioner, of course, but Buck says the commissioner will likely take the supervisor's recommendations. I think I might get the use of the warden's camp. I'll make that my home camp. Then I'll build a line camp near East Carry and another on Lower Black . . ."

Jeff paused, sensing a change in Gaston's face. "She no good, that piece," Gaston said. There was no laughter in his eyes now. "That place no good."

Ernie looked up shrewdly. "You're planning to trap that pocket, eh Gaston? If there are beaver in there, what's no good about it?"

"No good, that's all," Gaston said stubbornly. "I see wolve that place."

Ernie grinned. "You wouldn't be trying to scare a young feller would you now, Gaston?"

"So," Gaston said grandly. He jabbed a stiff finger at Ernie's chest. "You don' think I see a wolve, no? Gaston he see track. Gaston he hear at night. Make a man's blood run col'. Thees wolve I think may be he got a charm. In Canada, I know thees kind of wolve. Thees kind we call a *loup-garou.*"

"Nonsense," Ernie snapped. "You Frenchmen are worse than Indians when it comes to that superstition stuff. A wolf's just a wolf and as for being afraid of a wolf, you might as well be afraid of a snowshoe rabbit."

"*Loup-garou!*" Jeff repeated the dread word. "That sounds pretty ugly. I don't know what kind of a wolf that is but I'll take my chances, I guess. That is, if you intend to stake me."

Ernie's shrewd eyes met Jeff's. He hesitated momentarily. Then he slapped his big hand to the counter. "I tell you, Jeff, you go into that piece and I'll back you for a hundred dollars." He jerked his head at Gaston and winked at Jeff. "And what's more, if you bring back that wolf pelt of Gaston's, I'll pay you just that for it. What do you say?"

"Right," Jeff said. "I'll take you!" He reached for Ernie's extended hand and shook it firmly. "It's a deal!"

4. A Call from Old Carrie

It was Warden Supervisor Charles Bascom's frequent boast that his was the best division in the State of Maine. This might be called a slight exaggeration but, none the less, Chuck's opinion was echoed by every last man under his supervision.

The twenty-four hundred square miles that comprises Chuck's division is divided into six districts. In each one of these districts resides a warden whose job it is to enforce game laws and protect wildlife.

The warden's job is an exacting one. It is a job that calls for patience, courage and, most of all, judgment. Having in his charge an average territory of four hundred square miles, he cannot afford to use his authority irresponsibly and make enemies. He must be liked and respected to be effective. On the other hand, his uniform represents the dignity and the sovereignty of the state and he cannot permit himself to be demeaned.

The warden's job is often a delicate one. Trained to understand the meaning of the legal term *intent,* he frequently finds it the better part of wisdom to seek beyond the mere letter of the law for the vision behind it. In many cases a few words of friendly advice will do more for the cause of respect for law than the imposition of a fine.

The wardens in Chuck Bascom's division were required to be a great deal more than mere law officers. In fact, if a man came to Chuck with the idea of being a policeman and worked under the delusion that racking up convictions gave him prestige, Chuck soon put him straight on that point in no uncertain terms.

"If you wanted to be a cop, why didn't you join the State Police?" was Chuck's favorite remark to the overzealous. "The way to get ahead in this division is to keep a good, clean district with a minimum of court cases."

By and large, the man who came into Chuck's division didn't need to be told what his job was. An applicant is thoroughly investigated before being accepted as a trainee. And before a trainee gets a district of his own, he has anywhere from a few months to a few years of duty, under a warden's eye, behind him.

Chuck had seen a lot of trainees go through his division. His country was a popular proving ground. It had everything — all kinds of terrain, all kinds of hunting and fishing, all kinds of people and just about every problem in the book. Some trainees were good and some were just adequate. Some he recommended and some he didn't.

Every so often, a man would turn up who was so extremely good, so all-around perfect for the job, that Chuck would move heaven and earth to get him for the first opening in his own outfit.

Such a fellow was Buck Larrabee. He had got Buck and neither Chuck nor Buck was ever sorry that he had. Buck was short and built like a beer keg. He had blond hair, baby-blue eyes and a wide, jack-o'-lantern grin. Buck looked easygoing — and he was an amiable fellow. But when he had a job to do he did it right and thoroughly. In pursuit of his duty, he was patient, dogged. He had the persistence of a hunting weasel and the stamina of a pack horse. Buck had come from the Allagash Country. He was a water man. He could handle a boat the way a cowboy handles a horse — as though it were a part of him. Buck never smoked, seldom swore. His only vices were minor ones. He loved chocolate bars and he chewed gum incessantly.

It was Buck Larrabee Jeff found with Warden Hibbs in the living room of the farmhouse when he got back from the village that day. Buck and Will, despite the fifteen years difference in their ages, had become close friends. Holding down adjoining districts, they frequently worked together in night patrol and were wont to call upon one another for help when it was required.

"You know me, Will," Buck was saying. "I'm not too

fussy about my own company. It would suit me fine to have someone at that camp when I cruise in of a cold winter's night — well, here he is now." Buck's grin broke wide as he spied Jeff there. "I guess it's about settled. Or have you changed *your* mind about going in?"

"I haven't changed my mind," Jeff said. "I've just settled it. Ernie Sampson is going to stake me for a hundred dollars. What's more, if I bring back that wolf, I get the hundred back."

Will took the pipe from his mouth. He looked mildly astonished. "The wolf? Wait a minute, son. Don't tell me you've been listening to some of those crazy stories that are going around. We've got no wolves in this state. Once in a while we get reports of a wild dog of some kind. What I'm talking about is this yarn about a wolf hunting around Black Lake."

"A *loup-garou*," Jeff said. "Gaston LaFleur was talking about it. He won't go into that piece. What I didn't find out is just what a *loup-garou* is supposed to be."

Will shook his head impatiently. "It's all nonsense! Those Frenchmen!"

Buck stripped the wrapper off a fresh piece of gum and plopped it into his mouth. "I must say I can't swallow this witch business, Will. Just a plain wolf is bad enough for me. If I took a shot at a wolf and missed him, I'd call it

37

bad shooting. Those woods French when they miss call the wolf a witch."

"A witch?" Jeff echoed in some awe. "So that's why Gaston is afraid of that wolf!"

Buck chuckled. "If you want to believe Gaston, there's only one way to kill a witch-wolf. A man's got to load a gun with a silver button. You never see the wolf again if you hit him with silver. The superstition is that the wolf is an old crone in daylight. At night, she's transformed into a hunting wolf. If you listen to Gaston very long you'll wake up screaming."

The phone summoned sharply at that juncture. Will, still shaking his head, moved off to answer it. When he returned a few moments later, his face was grave.

"That was Old Carrie. She found out you were here. She wants to know if you'll take something to Willy Whiskers when you go upcountry."

"I will," Buck said cheerfully, "if it doesn't weigh half a ton."

Will sucked on his pipe in silence a moment. "It's a letter, I gather. Old Carrie sounded funny."

"Funny?"

"Well, maybe what I mean — is uneasy."

"Old Carrie uneasy! Don't be silly. There's nothing this side of the River Styx that can frighten that old war horse. I'll call her back tomorrow," Buck assured him. Buck rose and clapped Jeff on the shoulder. "Hey, fella, if you and I are going in Saturday, we got some organizing to do. Can you be ready?"

"I sure can," Jeff said heartily. "I'll call Mr. Sampson and have him pack my stuff."

"Pack light," Buck warned him. "No fancies. This winter, it's going to be a question of eating to live, not living to eat. But I guess so long as Ernie is paying for the grub, he'll see that you don't get any extras."

"Not even any gum and chocolate bars," Will said slyly.

Buck grinned. "You can trust me to take care of that, personally. Chocolate bars aren't an extra. They're a necessity."

Jeff went to bed that night feeling a stirring excitement in his chest. This was the great adventure! Working a trap line was no occupation for a greenhorn. In that country, once the winter closes down, even the best woodsman in the world walked teetering on the brink of disaster. He knew why Ma Hibbs had been reluctant to give her consent. A wife of a warden knows that even the best sometimes don't survive. In sub-zero weather, one false step can mean disaster. In a raging snowstorm, the price of carelessness is very apt to be death.

Almost every year that Lake Country would claim a winter victim. When a trapper didn't return at his appointed time, it was the wardens who moved in. Sometimes they found the body of the luckless man. Sometimes the body was never found.

Was he ready for it? Did he have the toughness and the savvy? He was sure he was and did. He was at home in the woods. He seemed to be in tune with the wilderness. He was seasoned now in body and mind. That spring, he and Skipper Doggett had been permitted to attend the Warden School and soak up what they could. He'd picked up some information for his mind to feed on, but most important, he had learned canoe handling. That fall, Warden Supervisor Bascom had recommended him for a guiding license. He had taken parties of greenhorns into the woods. He had seen the mistakes men made. He had learned that in the woods, man's greatest enemy is himself.

Yes, Jeff White was sure that he was ready for the test. He was quietly confident that he could meet the challenge. If he was wrong about himself, he thought, with grim humor, as he dozed off, he'd soon find out.

5. The Phantom Cook

THE WIND was in the south and the lowering sky held a threat of rain the morning Jeff and Warden Buck Larrabee headed into the village to pick up their gear and supplies. The little buglike jeep scurried down the winding road. Buck, cap back off his forehead, his jaw working rhythmically, recapitulated.

"If we aren't held up in the village too long, we should make the landing before noon. And if the rain holds off, we'll make across the lake to the carry by three. Toting about one hundred fifty pounds apiece we should make it to the river in three trips. We should make it into the camp in two days. We'll have to work fast. A southerly storm at this time of year usually means one thing. It'll come off cold. The ice is due. We're living on borrowed time right now."

"Mr. Sampson said he'd have my stuff ready," Jeff said. "Do you have to stop off at Carrie's?"

"I called her and told her to leave her note with Ernie Sampson. That old war horse sure likes to make errand boys out of us wardens."

41

Jeff knew all about Carrie. She lived alone on an old run-down farm. Big, cantankerous and tough, there wasn't a man in the region who cared to stand up to her when her dander was up. She had a habit of keeping the wardens humping. Even Supervisor Chuck Bascom, a man not noted for timidity, would take for cover when she was on a rampage. Carrie knew her "rights" and she made no bones about exacting her due as a citizen. The wardens were called in every time a deer got into her beans, a coon in her corn or a bear worked her orchard. Despite her demands, the wardens were genuinely fond of the old terror and it was suspected that their affection was returned. At least no warden ever left without a cup of coffee or a piece of her famous blueberry pie.

Jeff said thoughtfully, "Do you really think Carrie's afraid of something?"

Buck shrugged. "Scaring that lady takes some doin'. When she didn't read the riot act over the phone, Will just naturally jumped to the conclusion that she wasn't herself and I'll agree with him there."

"Could it be," Jeff said carefully, "this — this witch wolf?"

Buck laughed, but to Jeff's intent ears, Buck's voice was curiously lacking in merriment. "I'd forget that wolf nonsense if I were you, Tracker. If Carrie starts

42

telling us wardens we ought to get in a supply of silver bullets, that will be the last straw."

Ernie Sampson came out to meet them as they drove into the yard of the establishment. Seeing Buck, he grinned. "If you're taking Buck in with you, Jeff, maybe I'd better throw in a book of trapping laws. The boys tell me he's a hard man to please."

"Don't worry about Jeff," Buck said easily. "But you might mention to Gaston that he'd better not try jumping the gun on the beaver season this year. I'm going to be camping on his trail."

The three set to work loading the cartons aboard. When everything was stowed and Buck was lashing down the tarp, Ernie said: "Jack Bailey just dropped by. You doing any police work in there, Buck?"

Buck paused. He looked wary. "What do you mean?"

Ernie smiled. "Jack tells me the State Police have every road and brook out of that country covered. They think Dobson's in there and that the first good freeze will drive him out. There must be a nice fat reward on him. If you tag him and don't know what to do with the money, I know a nice charity."

"Sure, I know. The Sampson Fur Company, the widows' friend. Want me to laugh now or wait until I'm down the road?"

"Nobody loves a fur buyer," Ernie said lugubriously. "Go ahead, get out of sight, Buck."

Buck slid in behind the wheel. He waved his hand and was about to tramp on the starter. "Hey," he said suddenly, "I came near forgetting. Did Old Carrie leave something for me?"

"Carrie? That's right, she did call. She wants you to look in on Willy and tell him to take care of himself."

"That's funny," Buck frowned.

"What's so funny about it?"

"Hasn't Willy been looking out for himself a good many years now?"

It was just before noon when they arrived at Green Landing. The last three miles had been negotiated over a narrow, fern-choked logging road that threatened to disappear entirely at each turn.

"The end of the line," Buck announced.

Jeff piled out and stretched his cramped legs. A brisk wind was blowing off the lake and nagging little waves sucked hungrily at the rocky shore.

"Most of our boats have been taken to the District Four warden camp for winter storage and repair," Buck explained. "Let's have a look-see."

The canoe shed was set back in a stand of firs. Buck opened the padlock with a key from his ring and kicked the door back. Racked up were three boats. Jeff made out

44

the sleek shapes of two light canoes and a lapstreaked Rangeley boat.

Buck slapped the bottom of one of the light canoes. "This nineteen-foot White looks sound. Heave-ho. We've got a ten-mile water stint and I don't like the looks of it out there."

It was a twenty-minute job, once the canoe was on the beach, to load her. Jeff fetched down the supplies and Buck saw to it that the canoe was trimmed. A badly trimmed canoe is apt to take water inboard and this, Jeff knew, was the unpardonable sin to a water man.

At last Buck appeared satisfied. They returned to the shed and chose a couple of twelve-foot spruce setting poles and three paddles — one a spare. The poles and spare paddle were stowed under the thwarts. Then Buck produced a large sponge and tossed it into the stern.

He motioned Jeff into the bow. "We're off, Jeff. You take the bow paddle. Keep her steady into the wind now. We'll head for the lee on the west shore."

Jeff took his place on the forward seat and picked up the bow paddle. The frail boat shot out, scraping on the pebbles. Buck leaped aboard. Together their paddles bit into the water. The canoe lunged forward into open water. They were off!

Jeff felt a great expanding exhilaration crowding his chest. As the shore retreated under the whip of their

45

paddles, he thought of his friend Skipper Doggett. Skip, his adventure-loving companion of last fall's great, ill-starred camping trip. The slight irrepressible Skip with his penchant for whoppers would make a good wilderness side-kick. Jeff would have liked Skip with him at that moment as he was crossing the threshold into a new world.

There was little more than a mile of open water in this southern arm of the lake, but the wind had churned up a considerable chop. They had barely got deep water under their bottom before spray began wetting their faces. The lee shore was obscured by low-hanging clouds. It was discernible only as a darker shape rising above the slaty waters.

As they neared the farther shore, a flock of goldeneyes broke off the surface and, circling wide, whistled low across their bow. Ahead to the right, between them and the point, Jeff spied a fish hawk planing in circles, his keen eyes seeking a target for his talons. Suddenly, he thought of Willy Whiskers. What a place to live! Was there anything so strange about a man making a choice such as this peace-seeking man had made? Then from Willy, his mind turned to another wilderness-seeker. Willy had escaped for peace. This Dobson had escaped into the wilderness from fear.

It struck him that Dobson's taking to the woods had

been a foolish thing to do. It was far easier for a man to lose his identity in the thronging city. The very solitariness in this wild land made him a marked man. A man could starve in the city without much heed from his fellows. In this country a strange face or even a strange track could not go unnoted long. The wilderness was no place for a man to hide.

His thoughts were interrupted by a shout from Buck. "Hold her steady now, there's trouble ahead! Let's not ship any more water than we have to."

Jeff saw what he meant. Beyond the point the lake opened up and the steadily freshening wind had scuffed up racing whitecaps. It was going to be rough going when they cleared the point until they reached the quiet water beyond.

Wind and water came full upon them as the boat cleared the point. At once the fight was on. Jeff, his eyes blurred by driving rain, struggled to keep the bow into the wind. The frail boat pitched and yawed but the flashing paddles drove it on.

Jeff was ready for a respite when they slid into the calmer water of the river. He stretched his back and glanced around at Buck. Buck winked. "We made it, partner. You wield a good paddle. Let's beach and check our load."

They nosed into the small cove on the left bank and

hauled the canoe ashore. Buck laid aside the waterproof tarp. They found the load in good shape although there was considerable water in the bottom.

"A little water'll be good for her. She's been racked up for some time and needs limbering up." Then Buck glanced at Jeff with a half smile on his lips. "The first lesson in canoemanship is never to go out in water like that."

Jeff was just at the point of stowing his twelve-gauge when he straightened up. Buck had heard the sound, too, for he grinned. "There come some in around the bend. Blacks probably. You've still got two days to go on ducks. Let's see you get our supper."

Jeff dropped to one knee beside a screening shrub. Then he saw them. A foursome of blacks nosing down to land. Jeff's gun was hard at his shoulder and swinging. The gun spoke twice. Two ducks wheeled. There were two ducks floating on the surface of the shoal water.

Buck whistled. "That's a nice gun you've got there, Tracker."

Jeff laughed: "How about the fellow behind the trigger?"

"Gorgeous," Buck agreed. "Couldn't have done better myself. Shall we eat them here or push on to the carry?"

"Let's push on. I'm all set up for another ten miles."

They pushed out into the stream, picked up the floating

48

ducks, and once more the rhythmic swish of paddles was the only sound to break the silence. The river twisted and turned, cutting deep into the shore bank, first on the left and then the right. Now and then they spied a swimming muskrat, his nose making a furrow across the smooth water. Now and again a flashing jay went protesting across the stream in front of them to light in a tree at a safe distance and nag them out of sight. Accompanying their passage now was a band of merry little chickadees. Unlike the jays, these little black-capped songsters seemed pleased to see them.

Suddenly he felt Buck's paddle brake. A low whistle came from the stern. Jeff swung and saw Buck's eyes intent upon the west shore. Then Jeff heard the plaintive bawl of a cow moose. It seemed to come from just around the bend.

Buck motioned ahead and together they paddled stealthily around the next point. They came into view suddenly. A large cow and her calf were feeding in the marsh grass. The cow's head was raised, water dripping from her protuberant lip. She sent a blatting alarm echoing through the woods. Almost at once, Jeff was startled by an answering bellow, deeper and more menacing. Right before them, scarcely a canoe length along the east shore from where they waited, a giant black bull emerged from the forest wall.

Jeff, forgetting himself, whistled in amazement. The cow and the calf had moved leisurely for high ground and were gone. But the towering bull remained standing motionless, glaring at them balefully. At length, he too departed. Offering them a scornful snort, he wheeled off into the dark of the trees.

A mizzling rain was wetting their faces as they came into the quickening water of the shallows. Far ahead, Jeff heard the low roar of tumbling water.

"The falls," Buck said. He reached down and took up the setting pole. "You stay balanced in the bow and have a free ride," he said. "Use the paddle when there's any water under us."

Buck rose and placed his feet across the floor of the canoe and then set the pole into the gravelly bottom. Jeff half turned to watch Buck's pole work. His hands were placed high and each time the pole was set, his weight would drive the canoe forward. He kept the bow headed up with a delicate touch, using the gunwales as leverage or holding the pole wide and hauling the stern towards his set. It appeared to take no great effort at all to keep the craft driving upstream through the swift and shallow water.

To the left a small bite of beach opened up, and Buck headed in and beached the canoe. "We've done our day's stint. We'll make camp here," Buck said.

They slept that night under a fir bough lean-to with a night fire at their feet near the opening. Dawn came too soon for Jeff's tired body. It seemed he had barely dozed off before they were up and on the river once more.

They pushed on all that day with only a brief break for a noon meal. Night was coming on again when Buck jerked a thumb towards the west shore.

"Here is the start of Little Beaver Carry. It's short but a man-killer. Shall we camp here tonight or carry through?"

Jeff said, "I know what you'd do alone. You'd carry through."

Buck nodded. He uncoiled a couple of tumplines — leather straps that go across the forehead and tie under the load — and without further word he began unloading and arranging the packs.

"The tumpline is an Indian rig. White men don't use one as a rule. But personally, I haven't found any better way to carry a portage load."

The first part of the portage seemed simple enough, the trail winding upward at an easy grade. Then, with Buck in the van, they began the real haul upward out of a gully. The sweat began to pour freely from Jeff's forehead, stinging into his eyes. His breath came hard and fast as the load took its toll of nerve and muscle. Up and up the trail led and down and up again.

Suddenly a grateful breeze came freshly against his face as they came over a crest. There, through the trees, the lake showed like a welcoming beacon. Ahead, Buck slipped out of his load.

"Back and at it," Buck said with a grin. "If a man rests before this job is finished, he's apt to stay down."

Jeff shook out of his load and flipped out his red bandana, mopping his brow. "Did you tell me that was only one hundred and fifty pounds I was lugging?"

"I started you out with just under one hundred," Buck said. "You want to try for a hundred and fifty this time? Gaston LaFleur tells me that in his country one fifty is generally considered a 'man's load' on a portage."

"I'll try for a hundred," Jeff said grimly. "My legs are so numb they wouldn't know the difference."

Darkness was settling down when they made the last arduous trip, Jeff with the blankets and sleeping bags, and Buck bearing the canoe on his back, looking for all the world like a giant beetle.

Jeff dropped down prone upon the grass of the clearing. His muscles ached and the taste of blood was in his mouth. There was a burning sensation at the base of his neck from the backward tension of the tumpline.

He turned his head and saw Buck comfortably seated on the ground with his back against the canoe. Grinning, he extended a stick of gum. "You passed your first test as a water man, Jeff. Now all you've got to do is run the quick water in Devil's Run tomorrow and you get your papers. Hungry?"

Jeff sat up and reached for the gum. He stripped off the wrapper. "I guess it's the sign of a greenhorn to ask. But just how far is it to your camp from here?"

Buck laughed outright. "How far can you spit, Tracker?"

Jeff glanced around him, startled. He saw it then. Set back in a stand of birches stood a small log cabin, its roof splits so weathered and indistinguishable from the surroundings that it had escaped his eyes.

"We're here!"

"We're home," Buck agreed. "She's not much to look at but she's snug and sound."

Buck rose and made an expansive gesture toward the camp. His hand was arrested in mid-air. Jeff was aware at the same time that all was not as it should be. The acrid smell of wood smoke wrinkled his nostril. Then he saw the thin spiral of smoke issuing from the sheet-iron smoke pipe.

"We've got a visitor," Jeff exclaimed.

Buck was already sprinting towards the door. He was standing just inside when Jeff came up and there was a dark and puzzled expression on the warden's face.

Jeff was standing in a room about fifteen feet square.

There were two pole beds along one wall, a table made of puncheons — broad split logs — and several handmade chairs. There was a stove in a box of sand in one corner. There was a fire in the stove. On the stove in a frying pan some meat was sizzling.

And that was all there was in that room.

"Now that's real peculiar," Buck said softly. "A phantom cook."

Jeff had moved over to the stove. The meat had just begun to stick and burn. He removed the pan from the fire. "Say, that looks to me like venison."

"Whatever it is," Buck said, "I still call it doggone peculiar."

6. The Strange Visitor

IT TOOK only a quick glance to conclude that the camp had been occupied for several days and, judging from the stack of split stove wood, the shy interloper had been prepared for a considerable stay.

Buck continued to scan the room carefully, his jaw working, his blue eyes betraying nothing. He walked over to the double shelves in the stove corner where a few battered tin dishes were racked. He rubbed his hand across the shelf boards thoughtfully.

"There's nothing missing so far as I can see except that razor. That's where I kept it. I can still see the rust mark. And where is that pair of scissors I hung on that nail?"

Jeff said: "The door wasn't locked. Anyone could have got in. Don't you ever lock this camp?"

"And replace windows or repair door hinges every trip in?" Buck said wryly. "Nothing's locked up from here on in, Jeff. The men who go beyond the highways have learned to stick together. It's what you might call healthy self-interest. Your cabin's left open for the other guy because you don't know when you're going to get caught out in a winter storm and need the other fellow's diggings. There's a kind of a code that goes with it, though. A trapper who might steal from his own mother wouldn't think of robbing a wilderness camp. He leaves everything as he finds it and, if he uses up some firewood, he replaces it before he leaves. This stranger of ours doesn't belong in this country."

"Dobson?" Jeff whispered.

Buck shrugged. "Maybe. If it's Dobson we won't see any more of him tonight. We might as well get organized. I'll fetch in the gear while you cut us some fir bedding. There won't be much more light."

The rain was thickening and the wind rising to a lion's roar in the spruces as Jeff struck out into the thicket along the lake shore, ax over his shoulder.

He found a huddled clump of firs hard by and went to work. A pair of Canada jays — whisky-jacks or gorbies as they are commonly called by woodsmen — began flapping around above him in the trees, heckling him as he worked. Saucy, thieving rascals, they were the bane of the campfire life and, though every camper Jeff knew professed to dislike them, he had never heard of a woodsman who had lifted a finger to harm one of those bold, sooty-blue bandits.

It was all but dark when Jeff started back along the

56

shore with his load. A few rods from the camp he stopped. At his feet was a dark runnel in the gravelly beach. A canoe had been upturned there. Just beyond, he spied a boot track and beside it a bruiselike mark where a boat had recently been dragged back into the water.

When he stepped into the cabin, a wood fire was crackling in the stove, throwing fractured light over the cabin wall. Buck was up on a chair stowing bags of sugar and flour on the bracketed shelves close up to the eaves.

"So he left by water, eh?" Buck remarked without turning. "I figured he had."

"How did you know that?" Jeff looked startled.

"I saw you stop down below as I was bringing in the last load."

"He's got clean away," Jeff said. "A boat doesn't leave any track. If it's Dobson . . ."

Buck stepped down off the chair. "If it's Dobson, or anyone else, he won't get far tonight. It's six miles by water to Devil's Run. That portage is a man-killer even by daylight."

"Maybe," Jeff suggested, "he'll pole the rapids."

Buck snorted. "Pole Devil's Run? I don't know more than a handful of water men who'll try that in broad daylight with the sun astern. Look here, Tracker, I'm not a Canadian Mountie out to get his man. I'm out here to set up winter camp."

57

"But you said —"

"I said I was going to keep my eyes open. That's just a regular habit of mine. What say we eat and hit the sacks? We've got a big day tomorrow. It's going to come off cold after this blow. If we want to get out of here before the ice, we'll have to work fast."

They ate supper by candlelight. Buck had stewed the wild ducks with dehydrated vegetables that had cooked down into the gravy. The meal was eked out with the homemade biscuits Ma had insisted on packing and a pot of hot tea.

They were bent over the table, picking at the last bones, when a soft rap came on the door. Jeff looked questioningly at Buck.

"Might as well be camping in Grand Central Station," Buck muttered. He licked off his fingers and rose, wiping his hands on the seat of his pants. "Come in," Buck called.

They waited. The door didn't open. Buck called again, more sharply. Finally the door fell away. It opened slowly and, dimly revealed in the doorway, stood one of the strangest figures Jeff had ever seen.

A tall, shaggy, bearded figure stood there. It was not so much his face, concealed by tangled whiskers, that startled Jeff; it was his raiment that seemed so out of place on the shores of a wilderness lake. He wore a black coat that was cut off just at the knees. On his legs he wore a

pair of moose shanks — the hide of the hindquarters of a moose — that came up to meet the coat. On his feet were a pair of light moccasins.

He stood there, just inside the door, alert and taut as a hunted rabbit, his dark, gentle eyes ranging the room.

"Why, if it isn't Willy Whiskers!" Buck said cheerfully. "Come, make yourself at home, Willy. You know me. I'm an old friend of yours."

Out in the darkness a dog whimpered. "Down, Hunter," Willy said softly. He removed his old felt hat and grasped it in both his hands. "We are alone?" he asked.

"Sure thing, although we just seemed to have missed a visitor. Bring your dog in, Willy."

"Hunter likes it outside," Willy said. "He suspects all indoors. He was once abused by a man and there was no love in him." The strange recluse was looking inquiringly at Jeff.

"This is my young friend, Jeff White. I'll vouch for him, Willy. He's going to run a trap line in this territory. You can watch out for one another."

The man's soft eyes seemed to sink back into his skull. "Nothing goes unnoticed here: the death of a sparrow, the fall of a leaf; nothing goes unmarked, my young friend. I have come to tell you that evil is here. Evil has come to this innocent wilderness."

"You mean you have had a visitor, too?" Buck asked.

"I have seen the shadow of evil. I have seen the track of an unwelcome stranger. Something is lurking in the shadows. I know. Hunter knows. Hunter smells evil. Evil must not enter into God's wilderness. Be on guard."

Buck chewed thoughtfully a moment. "We'll keep our eyes open, Willy. Be neighborly, now. Sit down and have a cup of tea."

Willy waved his hand in polite refusal. The tall, unkempt recluse bowed again and, almost miraculously, the shadows absorbed him. He was gone through the door.

Buck came to his feet suddenly and loped after him. "Willy," Jeff heard him call. "Old Carrie had a message for you. She was going to send a note. But all I got was word to tell you to take care of yourself. Is that supposed to be a warning?"

Jeff, who had followed Buck to the door, saw the dark figure make a motion with one hand that suggested a benediction. "I need no help," the deep voice intoned, "I draw my strength from God's wilderness. Peace be with you."

With that he turned away. The ragged man, the shape of a great dog at his heels, moved into the woods and became a part of it.

Buck looked after him, rubbing his head. "Quite a fellow! What do you make of him?"

Jeff was still under the spell of the curious visitor. "He kind of gives me the creeps. He's not . . . ?"

"Dangerous?" Buck shook his head. "He may be touched, but Willy's one of the kindest men I've ever met. You can count on him as a friend if you ever need one."

Jeff was unconvinced. "I just hope I won't need one."

Sleep didn't come at once that night. They lay on their bunks looking up at the roof. "I've been thinking about Willy," Buck said thoughtfully. "All the years I've seen him in this country I only got close to him once. He talked for hours that day. He's read a lot of books, Willy has. He knows a lot of stuff."

"What kind of stuff?" Jeff wanted to know.

"Well," Buck mused, "about beaver for one thing. About history. There was a lot of blood shed over beaver back in history a way. It was like a gold rush in this wilderness and all across Canada. The Hudson's Bay Company got control first but then all kinds of rival outfits tried to cut in and pitched battles were pretty common. Between killing one another and slaughtering beaver for gold, it was a pretty mess."

"What did the Indian think about it?" Jeff asked.

"They traded peaceably at first, according to Willy. Then they saw what was happening. The Indian took only what he needed in fur for the winter ahead until the White Man came. The White Man showed the Indian what beavers could buy. Guns and trinkets and rum. At a white trading post a beaver skin was as good as gold, for its value didn't change. A beaver was what you might call par and it took so many other skins to equal a beaver. The value of a beaver was fixed at one dollar.

"After a while the White Man began to cheat. The traders got rich and greedy and wanted more and more furs for less goods. And Indian trappers had to bring in great bales of fur just to buy the bare necessities. Not only that, the Indians saw what was happening to their wilderness beaver. Beaver houses were being dynamited, dams blown up after the freeze. The beaver, not killed, died of starvation and cold in the ruins of their colonies. Some of the Indians tried to strike back and there were some bloody skirmishes. But the Indian, already softened up by civilization and White Man's rum, didn't have much of a chance. Both the Indian and the beaver fought a losing fight. Not too many generations back there was scarcely a beaver left in this country."

Jeff was thoughtful too. "I guess I can see why Willy hates civilization."

Buck was drowsy now. "You asked me once why I became a game warden. I've never thought about it much but I guess that's part of the answer with me. Only I figure we can have civilization without destroying nature to get it. I guess there'll always be wasters. A waster is just a guy who can't think about the future. The guys who do think about the future need help to hold those fellows down. That's what the warden's job is, Jeff."

"I never thought much about it either," Jeff said, "but I guess that's why I want to be a warden myself, some day."

7. A Grim Discovery

THEY WERE UP before dawn the next morning. Jeff knew by the tingling sensation at the tip of his nose that winter cold had come. He jumped out of bed and started up a fire in the stove. The kettle, boiling so merrily the night before, had a skim of ice on it. Glancing out of the window, he saw vapor curling off the glassy waters of the lake.

Jeff was holding his stiff hands over the stove when he heard the warden stir. Buck was rubbing his head and looking at him queerly.

"Hey, did you hear anything last night?"

"Not a thing," Jeff told him. "I slept like a top."

Buck looked sheepish. "Must have had a doggone dream. I thought I heard a wolf howl. I guess being touched is catchin'."

Buck leaped out of his bunk and took a look outside. "Tracker, we've got to move fast. I'd hate to think of getting caught in here. I've got a couple of fishing camps back of Duck Stream to check. I'll be back in about an

66

hour. How about getting your grub stowed while I leave the warden's calling card."

"Right," Jeff agreed, but he kept right on looking at Buck. "You aren't by any chance going out to look for a wolf track, are you?"

Buck snorted impatiently. "Nonsense, Tracker! Dream wolves don't leave tracks. Let's eat."

Buck departed right after breakfast and Jeff set to organizing the larder. The staples they had brought in were flour, rice, corn meal, salt, tea, pork, dried beans, and dehydrated milk and vegetables. When the food had been stowed on the high shelves, Jeff unpacked his traps and hung them on nails in the shed entryway.

He had about fifty traps in all, ranging in size from number ones to fours and fourteens. The majority of his traps, however, were number fourteens — which were the same weight as the fours, only equipped with teeth. This was the trap that Ernie had recommended for beaver. Half the beaver traps were packed to take into the line camp. Buck was going to help him set up on Black Lake. He also packed the emergency supplies that were to be cached there.

The sun, blood-red, was just bulging up over the lake when Buck returned to camp. "All seems right with the world," Buck said easily. "Are we set? We're going to see some white water today; we'll warp the canoe up, then carry around the falls. Tomorrow we might try to run it back if it doesn't look too unhealthy."

Ten minutes later they were on the lake. After three hours of steady paddling, shifting from right side to left at intervals, they were pushing up the reedy banks of Black Stream. Jeff heard the distant roar of rushing water. It was a sound that made his heartbeat quicken. The water under them was running swiftly over the shallow gravel bed.

Shortly, they both took to the setting poles. The tumult of tumbling water seemed just around the bend when Buck gave the word to beach.

A line was rigged. Jeff taking the right shore and Buck the left, they warped the canoe upstream through the racing water. Another half mile was accomplished in this fashion. Finally, the time came for the carry. They hauled the canoe ashore once more, unloaded it and prepared to portage around the falls to Black Lake.

"It'll be faster on the way back," Buck said, seeing Jeff's eyes fixed with excitement upon the rushing stream. "Well, what do you think? Do we run it tomorrow? This is a fine time to ask you if you can swim."

Jeff grinned. "I can swim. But I hope I don't have to prove it here."

It took several hours to carry into Black Lake. The day was waning fast when they had made the stretch, and Buck got out from under the canoe and Jeff from his pack.

"There are the remains of some logging shacks just below. They cut in here about ten years ago. One of the shacks might do for a line camp without much repairing. Let's have a look."

They proceeded unhampered along the shore. It was clear that a considerable lumbering operation had come and gone on the lake. Dammed for driving logs, timberland had been flooded; but now the water had returned to its original level, leaving a flowage border of dry-ki — dead drowned timber — around the shore. Most of the logging shacks were in a bad state and uninhabitable but they came upon what had once been a horse shed. Buck decided it could still be reclaimed and made to serve their purpose.

They started in that afternoon, working swiftly against the coming darkness. A curious bear had smashed in the door, judging by the evidence of claw marks, and porcupines had all but devoured the stalls.

"After all," Buck said cheerfully, "this isn't supposed to be home. All you want is a place to store some traps, a little grub, and a dry pair of socks. If you get hung up out this way in a northeaster, you'll appreciate the place a lot more than you do right now."

They ate a cold supper and turned in early on a bed

of freshly cut fir boughs. By dawn the following morning they had the shack in shape and were ready to proceed.

The sun gave no promise of warmth that morning as they made the portage to the foot of the falls. A rack of dirty clouds was building up in the east, waiting to way-lay the rising sun. A raw, cold wind nagged at Jeff's sweating body.

Buck looked concerned. "Snow?" Jeff questioned.

Buck nodded. "I'm afraid so. And after that — ice. This is about the end of open water. I'd hoped we might have time to do a little fur prospecting. There are live beaver colonies in all these flowages in the streams running into this lake. I've cruised all this country out from the air with the warden pilot."

"You said going back would be fast," Jeff suggested. "Couldn't we spare an hour, maybe, to look over the signs?"

"You've convinced me," Buck said with a laugh.

The cold was settling down. They slid into mittens and snuggled up shirt collars. Together they worked down along the shore with the thunder of white water pounding against their eardrums.

Game signs were plentiful. There were deer and moose tracks in the mud. A hundred yards downstream, Buck stopped to point out the print of a mink and, just beyond, the lacy track of a bounding weasel.

They worked all the way down to the dead water, then explored up a feeder brook. It was there that they came upon a beaver dam. The bright wood of the fresh workings indicated that here was a live beaver flowage.

The water of the stream had backed up, making a considerable pool. There in the center of the flowage, Jeff spied a mound of gnawed sticks and mud about five feet high and roughly fifteen feet in diameter.

A sharp sound like a hand clap startled the stillness. Buck laughed. "I thought maybe we might get a peek at a beaver at work. We won't now. The old man of the village just gave the warning with his tail. We might just as well cruise right along."

They worked their way back towards the main stream, following a deer path that meandered through a dense fir thicket.

Buck broke out to the stream and waited for Jeff to come up. He had a tight smile on his face as he nodded at the rushing water. "Changed your mind? Still want to shoot the riffles?"

"Let's go!" Jeff responded with an enthusiasm he didn't entirely feel. "It will only hurt for a minute, as Skip would say."

Without further word Jeff took his bow seat. Buck gripped the gunwales and shoved off. He was in his stern seat, paddle in his hands, as the current snatched them up, sucking the frail craft into the swirling waters of Devil's Run.

Once in the toils of the rushing water, everything else but the immediate challenge was swept from Jeff's mind.

This was the wildest stretch of quick water in the North Country and it had taken its toll in human life. Beneath them there was danger: rocks as cruel as shark's teeth lurking to rip at their bottom, swirling eddies waiting to engulf them, treacherous crosscurrents to snatch at their paddles or snag at their poles.

Buck was already standing in the stern, braking down the unbridled speed of the canoe. The forest wall slid by as the frail craft darted and careened on its twisting way among the boulders and over the riffles. The excitement caught in Jeff's throat. His impulse was to scream from sheer animal exhilaration.

It was a fight all the way. And then, suddenly, it was over. The canoe slid like a lazy porpoise into the peaceful water of the wilderness river.

Buck saluted with a grin. Stowing his pole he unpeeled a fresh stick of gum, picked up his paddle.

"A beautiful run, Tracker. You couldn't get a good drink out of the water we took aboard. Hold her in while I sponge out. I don't think we need to take time to check our load. We've got to beat this snow to camp."

They reached the warden camp on Secret Lake late that afternoon. The gray sky had lowered and a cold wind made a lonely cry in the spires of the black spruce; but the snow still held off.

That night the snow came. Huddled deep in the sealed warmth of his sleeping bag, Jeff heard the soft brush of snow against the roof. He dozed off, half believing that all this was a dream. Yet it was true. Here he was in body where his dreams as a small, city boy had once transported him.

And he thought, before sleep finally claimed him, of Luke White, his famous father, who had died by violence in this wilderness. It had been the memory of his father that had brought him back. He had helped to bring his father's killer to final justice. Once here he had remained to follow the wilderness trails in his father's footsteps.

Jeff knew as he lay in that wilderness cabin that the memory of his father would guide him all his life. To act and think as Luke White might have wished his son to act and think, would ever be a clear enough trail for him to follow.

The sound of a clattering stove lid awoke him. Jeff sat up to find Buck in his long underwear stirring up the fire.

"About eight inches," Buck informed him. "The lake

has slushed up a mite but we'll make it through all right."

There beyond the window lay a white new world gleaming ghostlike in the light of a gray dawn. As Jeff sat up, Buck reached out and massaged his tousled head in high spirits.

"An hour or two won't make too much difference. Let's cruise out and see what's moving in this fur pocket of yours. That is unless you'd prefer to stay abed."

Jeff eeled out in a flash. "How about using our snow-shoes?"

"Why not," Buck agreed. "I'd like to feel the old bats under me, myself."

They set out after a hurried breakfast into a world that was pure delight. Buck had showed Jeff the Indian snow-shoe hitch, a tie made with a leather thong that went around his boot from the toe strap, was made fast at the heel, and then half-hitched back on the binding again at both sides of the toe.

They had gone only a few hundred feet before the tracks began to show up. They crossed the fresh trail of a snowshoe rabbit and the delicate pronged track of a partridge furred with his winter shoes.

It was Jeff who spotted the fisher track at the edge of a fir thicket. The large forest weasel had apparently be-stirred himself early in search of a fat porcupine.

"Fishers don't bring what they used to," Buck said,

"but a few fisher skins will help your score. Hey, what's this?"

Buck had mushed ahead a few steps and was peering down at the track of a feeding deer.

"A doe deer just crossed over," Jeff said. "She doesn't seem to be worried this morning."

"Well, she ought to be," Buck observed grimly. "She's got an ugly surprise in store, my friend."

Then Jeff saw what he meant. Under the snow-weighted fir bough there was another print. There was just a dusting of snow under the bough. The four-toed track with its cloverlike pad print registered clearly and unmistakably. The small, furred fury of the North Woods — the wildcat — was on the hunt too.

Buck moved forward swiftly, waving Jeff to follow. Swiftly and silently they took up the trail. Reaching higher ground, the cat track swung away from his quarry to the west.

"He's circling to ambush. I've got an idea we're already too late."

Buck was right about that. Ten minutes later they came upon the wilderness tragedy. The cat, getting their scent, had departed; but there, stretched in the snow, still struggling weakly, lay a young doe deer.

The tracks told the story. The waiting cat had sprung from the ground to the luckless deer's back. The razor-sharp claws, sheathed in his stalking, had flashed out to their death-dealing work, ripping at the throat of the stricken animal.

The death ride had been brief. The last of the doe's red blood now stained the white snow. The deer lay still.

"That's another date I've got this winter," Jeff said. "I'll get that cat."

Buck nodded. "But on the other hand you need meat and you can't be too fussy about who did the killing. It's your meat, Jeff. Dress it out. You can hang that carcass high in its skin and you'll have venison most of the winter. You're not a real wilderness trapper until you have your frozen meat hung."

Jeff set to work. Unsheathing his small belt knife, he slit the skin from vent to stomach, taking care not to rupture the paunch. Buck nodded with approval when Jeff had completed the job.

"Good work. Couldn't have done better myself. Now Tracker, we've got to work fast and get out of the woods. Look at that cold sky. Ice is going to take hold tonight for keeps."

Arriving back at camp, Buck stepped ahead into the entry. Jeff, one arm braced against the log wall, was about to twist his heel free from the Indian hitch that bound his snowshoes.

In the fir thicket something crashed. It sounded like

a startled animal. Curious, Jeff readjusted his snowshoe and moved carefully across the clearing. He came upon the track first. It was difficult to identify it in the deep snow. Head down, he went deeper into the brush. His shoe nuzzled something half buried in the snow. He explored it gingerly. A chill of horror coursed up his back.

It was a man's boot! The boot looked gnawed as though it had been worried by sharp teeth. And it wasn't an empty boot! There at his feet, all but buried in the fresh snow, lay a sprawled body.

Jeff whistled, and his whistle was loud and shrill.

8. The Uneaten Supper

That was Dobson all right."

Warden Buck Larrabee slapped the wallet he'd been exploring and tossed it on the camp table. "He's dead; there's no question about that. What I'd like to know is how he got here. It must have been Dobson who was using our camp. He was quick to make tracks when we arrived. What did he come back for?"

"Maybe," Jeff suggested, "he wrecked his canoe after he left here and then got turned around traveling in the storm. Maybe he didn't know he was coming back here."

Jeff, still shaken by his grim discovery, sat stiffly on the bunk. He had emerged from his first shock. In the wood he had witnessed death in many forms. He had just seen a deer die, victim of a natural enemy. What was the difference, really? Yet he knew there must be a difference. But why did a human being consider his life more precious than that of an animal that roamed the forests?

Jeff, not naturally given to that kind of deep reflection, gave up. He had to admit, however, that he personally thought himself a little different from the animal, but only because he could sit there and think such thoughts.

Aloud he said: "Maybe it's just that a fellow doesn't expect to find a body of a man in the woods." Jeff frowned as another thought came to him. "And you certainly wouldn't expect a man to bother to shave in the woods, would you? He was freshly shaven."

Buck shrugged his bulky shoulders. "And with my razor, I'll bet. I guess the answer to that is simple. If he was planning to slip out of the woods and get away, he'd attract less attention shaved than unshaved. What about that money he was supposed to have stolen? There were only a few dollars in his wallet."

"And is there something else you're wondering about?" Jeff asked softly.

Buck looked over sharply. His revolving jaw stopped chewing. "Back on the wolf stuff, eh? Forget it. Will's right. There hasn't been a wolf in this neck of the woods since your good friend Gramp told his first whopper."

"What kind of tracks were they?" Jeff persisted.

Buck's eyes were guarded. "The snow was too deep and light for a clear register. It might have been any one of a number of animals. Say, we've got to get out of here. There'll be ice making on the lake tonight. Let's cover that body with brush and let the police make the next move."

Jeff remained thoughtful. He made no move to rise. "What about those teeth marks on the boot? Were they made after he was dead or before? Those were teeth marks, weren't they?"

"You noticed them, then?"

Jeff nodded. "And I noticed that you noticed them. Do you think — "

"Say, you're just as bad as your pal, Skipper. If this were the body of a hunter, I'd start thinking about it. This is the corpse of a criminal wanted by the police. If Jack Bailey wants to do some thinking about it, that's his privilege. All the same . . ."

Jeff glanced up quickly. "All the same what?"

"All the same — well, doggone it, how do we know that fellow died where you found him? That body could have been dragged there." Buck tossed up his hands. "There I go thinking again! Let's get out and cover that thing up and hit the paddle trail for home."

The cold was marrow-freezing, but there was little wind to cope with on the first day of the return journey. Steady paddling brought a warm glow to their bodies despite the tumbling temperature. Coming ashore at the end of the first day, they had to break through a crusty skim of ice that was forming along the lake edges.

Buck looked worried as they set about cutting boughs for a lean-to. "Are we going to make it?" Jeff asked.

Buck's grin was reassuring. "We'll make it. But we're not going to get out a moment too soon, I'll tell you that."

On a deep fir-bough bed, they slept huddled together for warmth that night. Jeff woke to find his exposed ear numb. A brisk fire and a snow massage of the damaged member fixed that.

Buck asked: "You still think you want to be a winter trapper? Wait until you get some cold weather. This is summer compared to what's coming."

Jeff smiled. "I'll let you know in the spring."

They pushed the canoe out through a slush of ice that gray and bitter morning. Although Jeff wouldn't have uttered his thoughts for the world, he was looking forward to that night when he'd sit down before one of Ma Hibbs's meals and turn into a warm, soft bed.

A dying glow stained the sky as they reached the last point between them and the landing. The lake was reflecting the last light of day when they drove the canoe through the slushing water and made a landing on the gravel beach.

Warden Buck Larrabee seemed strangely silent as he drove the jeep back along the rutted road. They were out on the gravel road when Buck said suddenly: "I think I'll stop by at Old Carrie's."

Jeff, drying out his wet socks on the car heater, looked

up quizzically. "You still are wondering what that message was?"

"I'm still wondering about a number of things, Tracker. Or maybe it's just that hers is the nearest phone."

It was well after nine that night when they drove into the barnyard of Old Carrie's run-down farm. The house was dark. As they climbed out, Jeff heard the restive stomping of the livestock in the barn. A horse whinnied softly.

Buck strode ahead and knocked sharply on the door. There was no response. He waited and rapped again. The house was still as death.

The warden gripped the door and pushed inward. It gave with a metallic creaking. It was unlocked. They stepped into the quiet house.

Purposefully, the warden took a flashlight from his pocket. Guided by its beam he strode on through the house into the kitchen. The stove was out. On the small kitchen table lay a plate full of food and beside it a cup of tea. They didn't have to move any closer to know that the food was ice cold.

Buck's boots rang out sharply on the floor. Jeff heard the phone click. Buck's voice sounded gruff and authoritative in the empty house.

"Get me Sheriff West. If he's not at his office, get him at his home. This is important."

9. The Surprise Arrival

Sheriff PARKER WEST hooked his hands under his red suspenders and slouched deeper into his swivel chair. "Boys," he announced with simple eloquence, "I need help."

He considered the wardens who sat negligently in chairs tipped back against the wall. He looked at the boy, Jeff White, who was sitting between the two, his hunting shirt open at the throat, his gunning cap in his hands. Neither Warden Will Hibbs nor Supervisor Bascom appeared impressed by the sheriff's plea.

Parker West sighed and took another tack. "Don't I co-operate with you wardens one hundred per cent? You boys brought all this trouble to me. Did I find a body in the woods? Did I find an old lady missing from her farm? All I ask—"

"Is a little time to go rabbit hunting," Chuck finished. "We don't ask for much either, Park. All Will and I ask for is a good night's sleep once or twice a month."

The sheriff looked injured. "Now isn't that a fine way

to talk to an old friend, Chuck. You talk like the Sheriff Department hasn't been doing a blessed thing. I've had fifteen men and twenty boy scouts combing that wooded area around Carrie's farm. But the snow came since she wandered off. We've got nothing to go on."

It was Will Hibbs's turn to sigh. "You got plenty of tracks now, if that's what you mean. You pull a hundred greenhorns into the woods, and when they've got everything tracked up like a barnyard you go and call for the wardens to help. Two good woodsmen might have found Carrie if she is in there. Now if you do find her, it won't be in time. Our whole division's been in there for three days. What more do you want us to do?"

"Well, boys," the sheriff said expansively, "what I've got is a problem in geography. With you boys in there, we'll find Carrie all right. It's this body. I don't rightly mind bodies when they're handy, but this body Buck Larrabee and the boy turned up is mighty inconvenient. Now *I* say it's over the county line and out of my bailiwick. I say it's Jack Bailey's body. Jack, who's just naturally cussed, says it isn't. Now if young Jeff here will point out on the map just where he found that body and maybe give the Sheriff Department the benefit of any doubt, I certainly would be much obliged."

Chuck slapped his knee and got to his feet. "Do that, Jeff, and give our sheriff the benefit of any doubt. It makes

88

no difference to us because you know what's going to happen in either case. The Warden Department plane is going to have to fly in." He grinned at Will. "Now we're picking up and delivering bodies."

Jeff was already standing by the wall map. His eye crossed the lake and moved along the thin line of the river to Black Lake. From there he worked back slowly. Jeff smiled inwardly as his eye rested on the broken line that indicated the county boundary. The camp, where they had found Dobson's body, ran right along the broken line.

Jeff's finger moved out and rested on the map. "It was on the far side of the brook here, Sheriff. I guess you win."

Will got to his feet grinning broadly. "And I guess from now on, Jeff, you can steal the church steeple and get away with it. You've made a friend for life."

Sheriff West was benign. He rose to shake hands all around. "All I wanted was the truth. I just wanted to be perfectly fair, that's all."

"That's all," Chuck agreed. "You just wanted to be fair, get re-elected and go rabbit hunting. So long, Park. Happy hunting."

Jeff had overslept that morning a few days later. The search for Old Carrie had continued with the wardens and the sheriff's posse in the wood from daybreak to dark. Jeff had stuck right with them.

He was still half asleep as he made his way to the kitchen for breakfast. Ma was cleaning up the dishes, and Pappy and Gramp were at the table in the midst of one of their endless arguments.

This particular difference of opinion concerned the raccoon and whether he did or did not wash everything he ate. Gramp's little eyes were fired with contempt as he slammed his palm flat on the table.

"It's ignorant people like you, you old skin-and-bones, that start that kind a foolishness. Why you ain't been farther out in the woods than the pasture for a year a Sundays an' the only sole thing you know 'bout a coon is that it tastes good with sweet pertatters!"

"Hush boys, hush!" Ma pleaded as Jeff stepped in. "Let's take a little time out to tell Jeff about the big surprise we've got for him."

Jeff's eyebrow rose. "For me?"

"You might say for all of us," Ma said mysteriously. "Anyhow, I'll bet you can't guess who landed in last night."

Pappy winked broadly and jerked his head towards the window. "One little peek might save you a heap of head-scratchin', Jefferson."

Jeff moved to the window. He let out a wild whoop. There, parked up against the barn, stood an ancient, battered model A Ford.

"Skipper! Skipper Doggett!" Jeff trumpeted. "Holy ole mackinaw, where is he?"

"Why, in the company bedroom, naturally. I made him let you sleep when he blew in late last night, and I think you might do the same for him."

"Not on your life!" Jeff was already mounting the stairs three at a time. He burst into the guest room. There was Skip deep in sleep, his rusty blond head buried in the pillow, one bare foot exposed over the edge of the bed.

"Hey!" Jeff bellowed. "Do you want to sleep your life away?"

Skip went right on sleeping. Jeff yanked off his blanket and snipped his naked foot. Skip drew his legs under his chin and twisting about buried his head deeper.

Then suddenly, as though a delayed message had penetrated, Skip squirmed about and sat up. "Jeff," he yelled. "Then I *have* come to the right place. How are you?"

Swinging his legs to the floor young Skip thrust out his hand. He winced as Jeff gripped it. "You've developed a grip like a steam shovel. Has Gramp been feeding you red meat?"

"I've been well taken care of," Jeff admitted. "Hey, what brings you here?"

Skip eyed Jeff thoughtfully. He scratched his bare

chest. "Well, let me see. Naturally, being a G-man, I can't tell you too much."

"Cut it out now," Jeff pleaded. "The least you can do is tell the truth."

"Then you don't believe I'm a G-man?"

"No."

"Well, you may be right." Skip sighed. His blue eyes brightened again. "How about just a plain Private Eye. You know, a Shamus?"

"A Shamus?"

"You know, a Private Dick."

Jeff tossed up his hands. "Try once more, will you? Right now you're just a public nuisance."

Skip appeared incredulous. "Don't you know what a detective is? That's simple enough, isn't it?"

"Sure. But you're not a detective. Look, you haven't got a hair on your chest."

"My best friend!" Skip said bitterly. "Even when I tell him the honest-to-goodness truth, he won't believe me. I suppose you want me to prove it?"

"That would help," Jeff admitted. "But I've got some more important business to talk over. You've come just at the right time."

"I like that! I suppose you don't consider running down murderers a serious business. Just look at this."

Skip bounced off the bed and began rummaging

through his opened suitcase. Triumphantly he produced a certificate and proffered it.

Jeff read: "This is to certify that Parker Doggett has satisfactorily completed the National Correspondence Course in Criminal Detection and Investigation. . . ."

"And it's signed by the secretary," Skip put in.

"This," Jeff asked doubtfully, "is supposed to prove that you're a detective?"

"It sure does! I've got all my equipment with me. When do I go to work? I read in the paper that you found a body. I'd like to go to the scene of the crime."

Jeff said patiently: "Nobody says it's a crime. And if you're going in there with me, you're going in to trap. There's beaver in there and fox and wildcat. I'm all set up to go in."

"Of course it's murder! It always is! I read about this case and I've got some theories."

"I'm still going trapping. But what I *will* do is call the sheriff and the State Police and tell them Inspector Skipper Doggett has arrived to take over the case. But first, I'd like to know if your mother knows you're out."

Skip feigned indignation. "What a question! Do you realize that I'm nineteen years old?"

"Seventeen," Jeff corrected.

"All right, seventeen. What's the difference?"

"Two years," Jeff suggested. "Maybe you should have

taken a course in arithmetic. So you didn't run away this time?"

"Don't be silly. When I was little, I ran away. Now I just leave for a little while. I always tell my family where I've been when I get home. Naturally, on this secret mission, I can't tell them too much."

"Then you don't think they'll mind your going trapping?"

"Listen," Skip protested, "I didn't say I was going trapping. What makes you think I'm going fifty miles into the wilderness just to keep you company? I've got my career to think of."

"You know how I know?" Jeff said with a twinkle. "I've just finished a course in fortunetelling."

10. Detective Doggett
Calls It Murder

WHAT WE'VE GOT to have, of course," Skipper Doggett said, "are clues. This is a very baffling case and I'm worried about it."

"What I'm worried about," Jeff reminded him, "are the beaver openings. What a fine mess if they didn't open up that country for beaver trapping, now that I'm all set up!"

Skipper put down his ax and sighed. "Wouldn't it be awful if it turned out there wasn't any foul play? And this my first case, too."

"Look here," Jeff put in, "we've got to finish bundling these Christmas trees. Pappy'll be back with the team any time now."

They went out on the hillside beyond the Hibbses' North Meadow, helping Pappy Newlin cut and bundle Christmas trees for market. They had cut a good many hundred that day, bundling them in the clearing for Pappy to team out to the road. There they were being stacked to be sold to a dealer who would truck them into the city markets.

"Clues," Skipper said dreamily. "What we've got to have are clues. The clues," he explained hastily, "always point to the wrong person; but that doesn't bother a really smart detective."

"What does bother a really smart detective?" Jeff asked patiently.

"Natural death," Skip said mournfully.

They heard the team coming in on the wood road and both the boys set to work quickly to finish the bundling. Pappy brought the bay team in over the light snow and backed the wagon around.

His battered old hat was down over his jib-sail nose. He was chewing contentedly on a match stick.

"Take her easy, boys; take her easy," Pappy drawled. "No sense in a feller killin' hisself with work. Jest take your time stowin' them trees. The sooner you get them stowed, the sooner I got to work."

In consideration for Pappy, the boys took their time loading up the wagon. Presently the load was aboard and lashed down; but instead of clucking the team into action, Pappy climbed down and lowered himself to an ice-rimmed log.

"I been thinking, boys," he said, taking out his pipe, his matchbox and tobacco tin, "that I ought to tell you some facts about this trappin'. I hate to think of you going on what that Gramp might a told you. Can't figure why it is but that Gramp jest naturally can't tell the truth. Now there's a right and a wrong way to do anythin'.

"Take smokin' a pipe, say. Now that Gramp, he'd smoke anythin' including moose droppings, and then he's bound to drive the load into his pipe like a wad into a muzzle-loader. Tobaccer got to be cut right and packed right. Finesse, that's what counts. That's French," Pappy explained. "Learned to speak it pretty good a way back when I was cookee in a loggin' camp.

Jeff watched with some dismay Pappy's elaborate preparation to light his pipe. It was getting late, and a cold wind was sluicing down off the mountain.

"About this trapping?" Jeff prodded him.

"Them 'good old days' of Gramp's!" Pappy snorted, "when wilderness trappers was wilderness trappers! Well, I ain't no octogenarian — whatever that is — but — "

"It means eighty years old," Skipper explained.

"He's lyin'," Pappy muttered; "but no matter how old he is, I can tell you some stuff that Gramp can't match, and it didn't happen no eighty years ago or even ten. Take that skeleton they found in a bear trap."

Both boys straightened up. Pappy, assured of his audience now, took his sweet time rubbing up his tobacco. He funneled it through his cupped fist into the pipe bowl.

"Up on Chain Lake they found him, both hands in his own bear trap. Now a bear trap ain't tender. It takes twenty-five pounds anyway to spring a bear trap. Everybody knowed that it was Blackie Barron's doings. This feller had been crowdin' Blackie's trapping territory and Blackie is no man to crowd. Blackie, he's as ugly a character as you ever want to see. They jest don't come any more downright mean than Blackie Barron."

"You mean to say," Jeff asked in horror, "Blackie put this man in his own bear trap and left him to starve?"

"That Blackie is a cold-blooded character. One little trick he had to take care of trapping competition was to go to a trapper's camp after he was gone and douse it good with salt water. When the trapper came back in the next fall, there'd be nothin' left but the stovepipe and stove."

Jeff looked blank. Then the light came into his eyes. "Porcupines!"

"Right. The porkies like nothin' better than salty wood. Oh, that Blackie, he's a black character, and he didn't live no eighty years ago. He went to prison. Never could get him for murder, but they did catch up with him for larceny. Picked up a logging company payroll one day. The Border Patrol boys nabbed him near the border."

"You don't mean to say he's wandering around now?" Skip asked uneasily.

Pappy struck the match on the seat of his pants and

was sucking the flame into his pipe. "If he's out a jail, I guess he knows better'n to come back into this country again. Now I was going to tell you about the right and proper set for a beaver."

It was Jeff who saw the car first. Beyond the clearing there was an opening to the North Meadow. He could see the road and the farmhouse. A car had come into the barnyard. He recognized the light blue sedan with its radio whip over the windshield.

"That's a State Police car! Maybe they've found Old Carrie!"

"Or maybe," Skip exclaimed, "they've got some clues for me to work on!"

"Now the right and proper way to set for a beaver," Pappy was saying —

But the boys, Jeff in the lead, were already breaking out across the meadow.

They were seated around the kitchen table when Jeff and Skip burst into the house. There was State Trooper Jack Bailey with a mug of coffee in his big fist. Chuck Bascom was there, helping himself from a plate filled with cookies.

Warden Hibbs in his work clothes was complaining: "Hey, this is supposed to be my day off. I should have gone out into the woods to hide."

"That's the only way a warden ever gets a day off,"

Chuck said. "Matter of fact, it was Jeff here that Jack wants to see."

"Me?" Jeff looked surprised.

"You found a body," Jack grumbled, "and a fine place to find a body, fifty miles from a lamppost!"

It was Skip's turn to look alive. His eyes were lighting up. "You mean you suspect foul play?"

Skip had come forward from the background. Jeff introduced him to the trooper and was about to introduce him to the warden supervisor when Chuck thrust out his hand.

"If it isn't my old friend, Skipper Doggett of the Junior Conservation Patrol. Don't tell me you're back. Haven't we got troubles enough?"

"Your troubles are over," Skipper said easily. "I'm now a detective, an expert in crime."

Jack blinked. Chuck winced. "I knew it! I woke up screaming last night. I knew something like this was going to happen to me. He's all yours, Jack. You need Detective Inspector Doggett a lot more than I do!"

"You've got troubles!" Jack barked.

Will laughed. "The only trouble Jack has is getting that belt around his waist."

"Would you mind taking your jokes outside for an airing. Come on in the other room, Jeff. I've got some pictures to show you."

In the living room Jack Bailey was suddenly serious. He took a stack of photographs from his pocket and shuffled them in his hands. He handed the stack to Jeff.

"Look them all over careful, now. Tell me if you recognize anybody."

He watched Jeff's face closely as the boy studied the pictures one by one. They were a strange assortment of snapshots, studio pictures, criminal-file photographs — all of men and each one of a different man.

Jeff, baffled by this procedure, was about to look up when he started in surprise. The picture exposed was of a square-faced man with close-cropped hair and cruel gray eyes. There was something familiar about that face, about the shape of the nose, the set of the eyes.

Then he had it. "The body! This might be Dobson."

"Sure?"

Jeff studied the photo once more. "I'm not certain, of course; but that jaw and those bushy eyebrows . . ."

"Turn it over," Jack said.

Jeff reversed the picture. There was a description on the back. His eyes popped. "It says here that his name is Blackie Barron."

"That's right. It looks like your Dobson is Blackie Barron. We found some fingerprints on the papers you and Buck brought back from the body. We sent them to Washington where they have prints of every convicted criminal in the country. They said it was Blackie. So I guess Blackie has come to the end of his career."

Will Hibbs and Supervisor Bascom had come into the room. "Smoky just called," Chuck said. "He says the ice can take him, and the weather report indicates a good ceiling."

Jack looked at Jeff. "What about it? Larrabee is busy on the Carrie hunt. Will you go in with me and the pilot tomorrow, and show me that body?"

Will clapped his hand on Jeff's back. "Here's your chance to go in like a modern trapper. They'll take the body out and leave you at your camp with Old Man Winter."

"Wait a minute," Skip had burst into the room. "You're not leaving me out of this. This is my first real body. My first honest-to-goodness murder."

Jack winced again. "Take it easy! I told you about my troubles. I got to go into the woods. I got to fly in an airplane. Don't make it murder. This guy is just dead, is all. Why has it got to be a murder?"

"Why?" Skip seemed surprised at the question. "Don't you read books? It always looks like natural death at first. Why — it's got to be a murder."

"I need a murder like I need a hole in my head. I got to get out of here." Jack started for the door.

"Don't pick on a nice fellow like Jack," the supervisor

pleaded. "The plane is only a three-place job. We'll get you in later. If Blackie's dead, I guess nobody's going to worry too much about how he died. Okay, Jeff?"

"You mean about going in? You don't think I'd miss a chance like this?"

"But why," Skipper persisted, "did Blackie, if he wanted to get away with that money, come into the one section of the country where he'd be most apt to be recognized?"

"Will you stop making riddles?" Jack snapped. "We don't need any detective. The body is dead, isn't it?"

Skipper Doggett sighed. "A fellow can practice, can't he?"

11. The Disappearing Body

DURING THE COURSE of his six years of service as a warden pilot in the Fish and Game Department, Joe "Smoky" Whitten thought he had done everything. One of six flying wardens, he had a good many hundred square miles of the state under the wings of his Piper Cruiser. He had seen many strange things and performed many curious duties. This, however, was a new one for Smoky. This time he had been requested to pick up and deliver a body.

The single-motored, three-place ship rose off the lake. He climbed to two thousand feet and leveled off, setting his nose for the notch between Sodunk and Lost Brother Mountain. Behind him the village was already swallowed in the haze. Ahead was nothing but hills and timber, lakes and streams so far as the eye could see.

Smoky glanced over his shoulder at the dark-visaged boy and the big, grim state trooper. "Better'n walking, eh? It took the old toe-pinchers six days to get in to trap. We'll do it in less than an hour. Anything in particular you want to see, Jack?"

"Sure," Jack told him. "A lamppost."

"Dogs use trees out here, Jack," Smoky said. "How about you, Jeff?"

Jeff was looking down at the serpentining river below. "I'd like to see some beaver."

"That's easy," Smoky said. "I've been beaver cruising for the past three weeks. The beaver reports have already gone to the supervisor. I don't mind telling you that Chuck's recommended that most of this country from here to Black be opened for beaver trapping, but it's up to the commissioner to give the final word on the openings."

"There are beaver all through here then?"

"Plenty. It looked bad ten years ago, they tell me. This wilderness country's more accessible from the Canadian side; and back some years, most of these flowages were poached out by aliens slipping over the border. Now that we've got planes to get in here, the pancake-tails are coming back."

"Won't trapping wipe them out again?" Jeff asked.

Smoky shook his head. "We haven't got all the answers yet for our beaver management program, but right now we feel that it's healthy to trap about six hundred beaver out of this division each year. If too many skins start coming out of one section, the commissioner has the power to close it right in the middle of any season. Do you think," Smoky added dryly, "there's a chance you and your partner might trap out your territory?"

Without warning, Smoky dropped altitude and circled back just over the treetops. He tipped down his right wing and pointed below at a small flowage on a feeder brook just up from the main stream. Then Jeff saw the beaver house and dam. He could discern where the snow mounded over the beaver lodge had been melted away by beaver exhalations. They were in that one all right. That was a live pond.

"Gaston LaFleur considers this his territory, so don't look at this pond too close," Smoky cautioned with a smile.

"I didn't think anyone could claim a territory, any more."

"You can't. It's first come first served, and I don't have to tell you that it's illegal to make trapping preparation on the ponds before the deadline. That gives everyone an even chance. Don't worry about Gaston. He's a big talker and a lot of wind."

Seeing the trooper's dour countenance, Smoky reached back and slapped Jack's knee. "Don't jump, Brother Bailey, we'll be settin' down in five minutes. You'll have your body."

"What I'm trying to figure out," Jack said, "is where I'm going to have it. In my lap?"

Smoky chuckled. "If you like. But I've brought a tarp along to wrap it in."

Secret Lake showed up white just ahead. They were winging low over the west shore when Smoky pointed down with his thumb. There was smoke coming from a half hidden camp on the edge of a handkerchief-sized clearing. A pattern of shoe tracks was laced around the clearing.

"Gaston's in. That's all the company you'll have for a while, if you call Gaston company. It's three miles across to your diggings."

A moment later the light plane cleared the lake and circled back for the landing. The trees, the snow-covered lake, rushed up to meet them. They struck once, twice, then skidded to a sharp halt in a flurry of snow.

They climbed out onto the lake. Pulling on his parka over his red winter jacket, Smoky tested the snow which had settled since Jeff's first trip in. Now there appeared to be something less than five inches on the lake.

"We won't need our snowshoes," Smoky decided. He turned to Jeff. "You lead the way. Got your bearings?"

Jeff nodded. "I found the body in that thicket just to the right of the camp."

"Right," Smoky said.

The weather was still unsettled. The cold was intense,

and overhead, ragged squall clouds swept across the sky, driven by a northwest wind. Jeff, in the van breaking trail, led the silent procession across the ice.

It was big Jack Bailey who broke the silence. He was breathing hard. "I always figured that any place you couldn't go in an automobile just wasn't worth seeing. Now I know it. A man's supposed to be civilized, isn't he? What's he want to go messing around out in this kind of country for?"

"Some people do things just to annoy cops," Smoky said briefly.

Jeff struck into the woods just above the camp clearing. He stopped, then rushed forward. Already he knew something was wrong. The brush and stone they had piled that day over the remains of Blackie Barron lay strewn and flattened under a blanket of snow.

He was standing there on the site of the surface grave. Only it was no longer a grave. He turned to the two men who had come up behind him.

"It's gone," Jeff whispered.

"What's gone?" Trooper Bailey asked. "You don't mean that body?"

"Here is where we left him. He's not here."

"He was dead, wasn't he?" Jack demanded. "What *is* this? That's no way for a body to act."

Smoky, who, like all warden pilots, had been a ground

warden first, was searching the terrain with an expert eye. Jeff saw where a few foxes had made an inspection tour. Just below, a snowshoe rabbit had left his trace on the snow. There was nothing else.

Smoky answered Jack's unspoken question. "I'd say the body was moved by a man. In the wilderness, no matter what we'd like to think, a body's carrion. It might have been a bear, but I doubt it."

Jeff's lips were dry. "How about a wolf?"

"A wolf!" Trooper Bailey's head came up. "Look, let's get out of here."

Smoky snorted. "Brother Jeff, forget that wolf stuff. I heard what Gaston told you. Don't you know he's just trying to put a scare into you boys? You've got a rich fur pocket here and you're too close to Gaston for his comfort." He fanned out his hand at the trooper. "It's your move, Jack. I'm just here for the ride."

"What do you expect me to do without a body? I'm calling it a bear. Blackie is dead, isn't he? We got his fingerprints off his papers, haven't we? All I say is that bear must have been mighty hard up to pick on Blackie Barron. Let's get out of here."

"I've got some venison hung," Jeff said. "We can stop over at the camp and fry up a meal first."

Some light returned to Jack's eyes. "No matter what happens to me, somehow I can always eat."

Back at the warden camp, Jeff cut off some venison. A fire was started and a frying pan set on the stove to heat. They fried up a platter of meat and set to like a pack of hungry hounds.

Smoky took his cup of tea to the window and scanned the sky. "We've got to head back. I don't like the look of it up there." Then he glanced at Jeff. "You sure you want to stay in?"

Jeff nodded. "Why not?"

Smoky merely shrugged. "I don't know why not. I guess you can take care of yourself."

Jeff knew what was stirring in the pilot's mind. He smiled a little. "Whatever you do, don't tell Skipper Doggett you don't like the bear story. I've got to live with him."

"Look," Smoky said. "I'm not thinking anything. All I'm doing today is flying that crate out there. Let Jack do the thinking."

"It's a bear," Jack said, mopping up his plate. "Look, use your head. Who'd want a body but a bear?"

"Your boss," Smoky suggested. "But he's your boss, not mine."

Long after the plane had droned off into the distance that afternoon, the sound remained like an echo in Jeff's ears. He was alone in the wilderness. A strange sweet loneliness took hold of him as he prepared to eat his evening meal. He was alone. It was hard to believe how alone he really was.

He turned in early. He lay awake for a while hearing the nerve-tingling sound of ice making on the lake. Across the water a fox yelped; from a neighboring thicket he heard the cry of a hunting owl.

This was the beginning. Did he have the strength and the courage to meet the challenge of the wilderness? He thought of his father, and he was sure that he had.

12. Wilderness Christmas

THE NEXT MORNING was cold and blustery. He saw that some three or four inches of snow had fallen during the night, filling in the tracks of his departed guests. It looked like a good day to don snowshoes and do a little beaver-cruising.

Cleaning up his breakfast dishes, Jeff saw a small gray lump on the floor in the corner. Upon closer inspection he found that it was a dead field mouse. It seemed to Jeff at the moment like a rather silly place for a mouse to die. He disposed of the luckless rodent without ceremony, tossing him into a snow bank beyond the door.

Parka zipped up to his chin, mittens on his hands and a light pack on his back, Jeff hit the trail with the first light. Although it was illegal to make trapping preparation before opening day, Jeff reflected, there certainly was no law against cruising out the flowages and planning his set sites.

And too, the more he could learn about the beaver, the more successful he would be in taking fur. He knew considerably about the little wilderness engineer from what he had read and he had learned considerably more from listening and questioning. But most valuable was the lore he had gathered himself while watching a beaver pond, lying flat and still in the screening swale grass.

And he had learned a great deal from Warden Will Hibbs who had spent all his life observing wilderness ways. After a beaver is two years old, he is driven from the home lodge, and it's up to him to mate and make a home for himself. This eviction usually happens in April. The young beaver works upstream or down, looking for a likely spot. He looks for a site with ample food — poplar, birch, hemlock and the roots of marsh vegetation.

The site chosen, he and his new mate, perhaps with some help from the old man, construct a dam to create a good-sized pond where he and his family will be able to store food under the ice and find room to move about for titbits. He will also choose a site with a high bank in which he can dig out bank dens where a good part of his underwater life will be spent.

Dams are built of both live and dead wood. After the dam is raised, a particularly cautious beaver will construct several counter dams below the main obstruction for extra assurance of the proper water level for his well-being.

Jeff had watched the spring antics of the beaver. He had frequently come upon the beaver "mudpies" on a stone. It is upon these mud pancakes that the young beaver out on his own puts his scent, indicating to any eligible that he's ready to mate and settle down.

Jeff knew how to check the beaver cuttings around a live flowage to ascertain how many beaver were living there. This was a part of beaver-cruising. He knew from what he had heard and seen that an average beaver family consists of seven to nine beaver, two adults and the rest mostly yearlings or kits. The lodge is composed of the same materials as the dam, and it takes an average work group about two weeks to construct one. Attached to the lodge is a feed raft fastened underwater by an entwining of roots.

It was along about noon of that day that Jeff, working up an ice-sheathed stream, came upon his first live beaver flowage. He stalked in cautiously, knowing the greenhorn trapper's mistake of making careless preparations and putting the colony on its guard.

This was a large house and, judging from the cuttings around the pond's edges, it harbored an oversize family of twelve or more. He inched out on the ice, his narrowed eyes considering possible sites for his sets.

He had decided to use what was termed locally as a chair set. He would chisel a hole in the ice large enough to accommodate a six-inch log and leave room to work and inspect the underwater set. A chair or stick platform would be nailed or wired to the pole on which the trap would set. Above the platform, faggots of poplar would be wired on for bait. The hole cut, he would work the log down into the mud, push snow around the opening to prevent it from freezing over, then depart as quickly and quietly as possible.

He studied the scene, trying to decide where the beaver runs might be. It was illegal, he knew, to trap within twenty-five feet of the lodge. The old trappers never trapped so close anyway, for near the lodge all you were apt to get were the kits and yearlings who never wandered far from home.

His plan in mind, Jeff made a note on his map and sat down on a log to consume his meager noon meal. Later he worked upstream, found a spring hole and knelt for an icy drink before proceeding on his way.

He worked all the way to Black Lake that day. There, cold and exhausted, he rolled in for the night without bothering to light a cook fire. The wind had fallen off but the cold had deepened. The old drum stove he and Buck had rigged up for heat went out several times during the night. Jeff was up stiff and cold long before dawn, and resolved to be on his way.

That morning he found another large beaver colony just below the dam on the east side of the stream. Tallying up, he found he had located ten live beaver flowages, making roughly a total count of eighty beaver. That looked good. That looked very good. He and his partner Skip had their work cut out for them.

Arriving back at his home camp late that day was like coming home. What had appeared, on his first introduction to the warden camp, like a rude hovel now seemed a mansion with all the creature comforts a man could desire. He cooked a meal that night large enough for a dozen men, it seemed, and he ate it down to the last scrap.

He was busy the next few days. In addition to beaver cruising, there was wood to cut and stow, the camp needed chinking in spots and he had to go some distance to find a spring hole that would produce enough moss for the job. There were his traps to sort and prepare and clean. He tried not to think of Willy Whiskers and his direful warning of evil, and so occupied was he that it took little effort to keep forebodings from his mind.

It was only when the wind howled in the stiff-limbed tree at night that his thoughts took a dark turn. More important right then was a small domestic mystery. He had found another dead mouse, and the next day a third in almost the very same spot.

The following night the mystery was solved. He heard a stirring, a small squeal and then silence. He had just dozed off but the sound brought him erect on his bed. The moon was almost full and in the wash of light that entered through the small window he saw a flash of white.

Jeff laughed aloud. He knew the answer then. He had a friend rather than an enemy. Through some tiny chink, an ermine — the small winter weasel — had been entering nightly for mice. The weasel, the most efficient killer in nature's kingdom, had been doing a good job.

"So now," Jeff thought as he fell off to sleep, "I've got some company for the long winter evenings."

But search as he did, that next day, for the weasel's entry, he could find no trace of it. That mystery he never did solve.

About a week later — Jeff had lost any accurate accounting of time — the warden plane flew in with Skipper Doggett.

Jeff rushed out of doors at the sound of the low-flying plane. He waved in the clearing as it circled low and came slanting out of the sky to set down on the frozen lake.

He met them warmly as they came off the lake, young Skip with a laden pack basket on his back, and Warden Pilot Whitten bearing a large beribboned package.

"How's Ma and Will and Gramp and Pappy? How's everybody?" Jeff wanted to know.

"Hey, one at a time!" Smoky pleaded. "Everybody's wonderful and everybody wants to say Merry Christmas to you."

Stomping ahead into the cabin, Skipper tossed off his pack. "Golly diamonds, it looks to me as though some dirty old trapper's been living here! Quite a joint."

"There'll be two dirty trappers living here from now on. Hey, what's this about Merry Christmas?" Jeff asked.

Smoky set the package on the table. "There it is. Don't you know what date this is? This is Christmas Eve and Santa gets around by plane now."

"Well, what do you know!" Jeff exclaimed. "Merry Christmas! Hey, let me put another log on the fire and brew some tea."

"And look here," Skip said, "how about a Christmas tree? I'll run right out and cut us one."

When Skip had dashed through the door with an ax in his hand, Jeff swung to the warden. "What about the big news? Is it fox and bobcat or are we going to get a chance at those beaver?"

Smoky was flexing his stiff hands over the stove. "You're in, boy," he said. "The openings were published last week. It's open for beaver trappers from just below here all the way up to Little Squaw. I'm afraid Gaston's a little out of luck though. Most of his territory is south and east of Secret. My guess is that you'll have company."

Jeff was elated. "I don't mind competition just so long as Gaston knows the rules. Do you think he'll jump the gun and make preparations?"

"I've warned him enough on that count." Smoky gave Jeff a tight-lipped smile. "You see that he doesn't," Smoky said.

"But I thought he was afraid of that wolf. He's the one who told me about that *loup-garou.*"

Smoky chuckled. "That's one way of discouraging competition, isn't it? Gaston's a sly one. The only thing Gaston is afraid of is not getting enough fur."

Jeff had the tea brewed when Skipper stomped in lugging a small fir tree by the butt. "Now all we need is a plum pudding," Skip announced.

"I can offer you some raisins," Jeff suggested. "I'll mix them up with some nice corn meal."

Smoky set down his tea cup. "Me, I'm on my way. I've got a Christmas waiting for me at home. Good luck, trappers, and keep your hands out of ice water."

With an airy wave of his hand, Smoky was gone.

In the doorway they waved him off as he cleared the treetops and gunned his ship towards home. Then the boys faced one another. Jeff thrust out his hand.

"Merry Christmas, partner."

Skip took the proffered hand in a hard grip. "Merry Christmas; may all our adventures be happy ones."

That night before the fire they opened the box. There were a new pair of mittens and a can of homemade cookies from Ma. Pappy had sent three pairs of wool socks and

Gramp a fleshing knife. The last present was from Will. Jeff opened it slowly, Skip's bright eyes upon him.

"I know," he said. "I'll bet you can't guess."

"I can guess," Jeff whispered, "but I don't dare to. I might be wrong."

But he was right! There, exposed now on the table, was a spanking new .22 Woodsman revolver.

"Wow!" Jeff shouted. "What a Christmas! Let's shoot her off."

"Sure," Skip agreed, "and let's sing Gaston some Christmas carols."

"He'll never hear us. He's three miles off, but let's have one anyway."

That night, their breath pluming whitely, they sang "God Rest Ye Merry Gentlemen" to the frosty stars. It was the strangest and most wonderful Christmas Eve Jeff had ever known.

13. The Curiosity Set

Hᴇʏ, wake up; we're snowbound!"

It was Skip's exultant cry that brought Jeff out of sleep the following morning. Sure enough, an all-obscuring snow was slanting across the single window. The wind, savage and shrill, whistled around the cabin corners.

"This looks like a good day to lay out our trap line on paper and bark-boil our traps," Jeff suggested.

Skip was slipping into his breeches. "Or," he countered, "study this case of the missing body."

Jeff groaned. "Holy ole mackinaw! Are you going to start that again? We're here to trap. As Smoky said, this Blackie was a scoundrel. Let's not worry about how he came to his timely end."

"Only now," Skip said evenly, "we've got two deaths to think about."

Jeff was checking over the stove. He straightened up. "Two deaths?"

"They don't expect to find Old Carrie alive, if they do

find her at all. You know we've got a real fifty-carat mystery on our hands, Jeff."

"I never heard of a fifty-carat anything and it's not on my hands. I'm here to trap."

Skip ignored the interruption. "The authorities are baffled," Skip pursued. "At the moment even *I* am baffled. Right now the authorities are looking for clues. I don't work that way. According to my book, the first thing you should look for is a motive."

"Well, this is certainly no place to look for one — out here. You're about fifty miles from a single motive."

"I'm not so sure," Skip said thoughtfully. "Have you an idea? Take that stolen razor, for instance."

"What's that got to do with Carrie's disappearance?"

"How do I know?" Skipper snapped irritably. "But just take it. You aren't busy right now."

"You take it. I'm going to be busy right now getting breakfast." Jeff threw up his hands. "Are you at all interested in beaver? I thought you wanted to be a trapper."

"I will be disguised as a trapper," Skip said. "Only you and the chief know I'm really Operative 23."

"Chief who, may I ask?"

Skip sighed. "Even I don't know who the chief is. I know him only as Number One."

"Snow or no snow I'm getting out of here," Jeff barked, banging the frying pan down on the stove. "You can stay here with your false beard. I'm going out to try my new handgun."

Skip was Skip again in a glimmering. "Why didn't you say so? Don't think you're going out and leave me here all alone."

But it was almost noon before they were organized and abroad that day. Jeff first set some of his traps to boil in bark to discolor and deodorize them for the trap line. In this job, Skip gave him a willing hand.

Their snowshoes lashed on with the Indian hitch, they broke trail through two feet of snow. Snow was still falling lightly, but overhead the storm appeared to be breaking up. They had traveled only a half mile beyond the camp when the sun emerged, making a blinding brilliance of the fresh white forest carpet.

It was Skip who came upon the cat track as they were crossing Hatchet Brook. Jeff moved over and nodded. "That's a wildcat, right enough. This is about the same spot Warden Larrabee and I picked up that cat trail. This may be *my* cat."

"It's not your cat," Skip suggested, "until you get him."

Eyes narrow, Jeff studied the terrain. "Cats have been traveling through here. I'll bet this is a regular cat run." His eyes came up. "Well, what do you say? If you mush back and pick up one of these number two's, I'll be rigging up a set for this fellow."

"Sure," Skip agreed, "but how about bait?"

"We've got no bait handy. But they do say curiosity killed a cat. Let's try it."

"Try what?"

"A curiosity set. I've heard some of the old toe-pinchers say it sometimes works on cats. One fellow told me about the cat he trapped with an unstoppered jug. He made a trail set and put a jug beside it. The bottle opening made a whistling in the wind. The cat studied the bottle for three days, and his curiosity finally couldn't stand it any longer. He went up to investigate and was caught in the trap."

Skip looked doubtful. "Maybe it was *your* leg that toe-pincher was trying to yank; but you're the boss."

While Skip was gone Jeff freed his belt ax. He cut and limbed out a dead cedar about eight feet long and six inches through. He placed one end on the snow and braced the other against a stout spruce about a foot above the snow line. He limbed off the spruce trunk above the log, and, shaking out his large red bandana, impaled it on a branch stub. Then he proceeded to notch out a platform for the trap on the dead log just beneath the dangling red cloth.

He stood back to inspect his handiwork. In theory the passing cat would be curious. Also in theory the cat would have to climb the slanting log to satisfy his curiosity. And, still in the realm of theory, the cat would step on the trap pan and be caught.

"In theory," Jeff thought, "I practically got that cat skun out."

Jeff had slipped into his canvas gloves ready for the trap when Skip appeared. He set the trap on the notch and sprinkled snow over it.

"Well, you've got me convinced," Skip admitted. "Now all you've got to do is convince that cat. Now what?"

"Let's work out a ways and try this gun." He considered the sky a moment. The sun had gone again. "But let's not get too far. This storm isn't over yet."

With Jeff in the lead they trekked up over the hardwood ridge. It was here that Jeff stopped quite suddenly. Just ahead of him, a fresh snowshoe track marred the wilderness snow.

Skip came up quickly. "It must be either Willy or Gaston LaFleur. There is no one else in here."

"Whoever it is, that trail comes from the direction of our camp. Let's get back."

The snow had begun to fall thickly again. An inexplicable foreboding took hold of him. The snow was driving hard now, stinging their faces. The tracks of the stranger were drifting in rapidly.

A half mile above the camp, Jeff saw where the tracks had crossed their own. A friend, he thought darkly, would have overhauled them for a greeting. It was too late to follow those tracks and answer the questions in his mind. Besides, in fifteen minutes, the way the snow was falling, the last traces would be obliterated.

Jeff reached the camp first. Quickly freeing his jacket, he clasped the cold handle of his gun and stepped through the door.

The cabin was cold — and empty. Skip at his side, Jeff stood there quite still for several moments, his dark eyes ranging the small room. Everything appeared as they had left it. His eyes fixed sharply upon a white lump of snow on the floor near the stove.

"We've had company," Jeff said.

"Golly diamonds!" Skip said uneasily. "Now you're the one who's getting all hot and bothered. Maybe it was a friend of ours. We've got *some* friends, you know."

"Friends don't wait until we've left," Jeff said softly.

14. Gaston Joins Up

THE NEXT SEVERAL DAYS Jeff and Skipper slept with one eye open. Jeff knew that it was useless to try to fool themselves. Someone, for some reason, was watching them.

As Skip put it: "No one could pick up any expert trapping pointers from us. There must be a *good* reason."

"Maybe," Jeff suggested dryly, "he's got wind of the fact that you're not a trapper at all but Operative 23 in disguise."

"Wait a minute," Skip protested. "This isn't any joking matter. Whoever it is thinks we know something. Why doesn't he show his face and ask his questions?"

They were clearing the breakfast dishes preparatory to hitting the trail that morning with a few more cat traps. So far Jeff's curiosity set had not produced a cat; but he still hadn't abandoned hope.

Thoughtfully, Jeff set the last dish on the back of the stove to dry. "I wish I could think of a better idea, but I guess all we can do is to wait for him to show his hand again. I have a hunch we're safe until it snows again."

Skip looked puzzled. Then light came into his eyes. "Golly diamonds, I think you're right. I'm supposed to be the detective. Why didn't I think of that? He'll come in the snow as he came last time. He wants no snowshoe tracks to betray him. He'll come when he knows that snow will cover up his tracks."

Jeff nodded. "Just the same I don't think we'd better split up for a while."

"Right," Skip agreed promptly. "It's much nicer to get murdered together, partner."

They struck out, planning to check the cat set and make several more sets on the side of Big Squaw Mountain. There were two days to go before the beaver season opened, and it seemed a good practical idea to both of them to devote the time to cats. The mountainside was also good fisher territory; and, although fisher weren't bringing the price they had in Gramp's day, they still were worth picking up.

"The fisher season doesn't open until next week," Jeff said, "but a good trapper, they tell me, spends more time prospecting than he does trapping. Let's find out where they're moving on the mountain."

"I don't get it," Skip queried. "They don't fish, and you don't find them near water. Whoever thought up the name *fisher?*"

"You got me," Jeff admitted. "But I remember Gramp

telling me that the fisher is a great hand at stealing fish bait from traps. The fisher's a weasel and a deadly killer. He'll eat just about anything, but a porcupine's his favorite dish. They tell me that a fisher's just about the only animal who'll fool around with a porcupine. He flips them over to get at the soft underbelly."

A low snarl stopped Jeff dead in his tracks. Jeff dashed forward. "Our set's just ahead. I think we've got our first customer."

A great cry of rage met Jeff as he burst into the opening. Then, with a hissing, spitting snarl, the trapped cat leaped into the air to fall thrashing in savage frustration in the snow.

Jeff dispatched him quickly and mercifully with a well-placed head shot from his handgun. Skipper, puffing hard, came into the arena.

"A beauty!" he exclaimed. "That curiosity make's some bait!"

Jeff freed the cat's foot and held him aloft. "He'll go forty pounds. And there, partner, is fifteen dollars bounty money plus whatever we can get for the skin."

"Why there's money in this business. We'll be rich if this keeps up," Skip exulted.

"Maybe," Jeff said, "we'd better not count our cats until they're skun."

Together they rough-skinned the cat on the spot and

packed the carcass for bait. They kicked up several snow-shoe rabbits in a fir thicket just above, and Jeff shot one of them. "If we don't use him for bait, we can always have a rabbit stew for supper," Jeff remarked.

Further up the mountain they ran into another cat trail. They made another set at a natural crossing. Beyond the trap they placed a piece of the cat carcass against the tree, covering it lightly with dirt and moss. Jeff drove two guide sticks to form a natural obstruction each side of the trap to force the cat to go over the trap for the bait.

They were setting their last trap when Jeff reached into his pocket and brought out a small medicine bottle.

"I forgot all about this bottle Gramp gave me. I brought it with me to try out."

"What is that, cough medicine?" Skip asked.

"Cat medicine. It's Gramp's own private recipe for a cat lure. Cats are finicky, he says, but this is bound to get them."

He uncorked the bottle and held it out. Skip took one whiff and winced. "It would make me run a mile the other way. Golly diamonds, what's that made of?"

"Didn't I tell you it's a secret? Gramp admitted there was fish oil in it and muskrat musk, some ground beaver castors and a dash of oil of catnip. The secret ingredient he wouldn't tell me."

"By all means," Skip said in disgust, "keep it a secret. I sure don't want to know."

They were about to stop for a trail lunch when Jeff saw the first fisher track. He spied it first on a log on which they were about to sit down. It looked like a large mink track except that the fifth toe seemed to have been added as an afterthought.

Jeff pointed to where the fisher had gone bounding off through the snow. "Let's make a date with that one next week, Skip."

"Maybe," Skip remarked, studying the track, "we'd best just not tell that fisher anything about it. Let's call it a blind date."

They were back towards the stream late that afternoon when Skip drew up. "Hey, what kind of a bird is that?"

Jeff stopped to listen. He heard it then. A distant *chump, chump, chump* registered on his ear. He frowned. It seemed to come from the direction of the stream.

Suddenly Jeff's jaw stiffened. "Come on," he commanded, "that's no bird!"

"What is it then?" Skip shouted after Jeff's running figure.

"That," Jeff called over his shoulder, "is an ice chisel or I'm a monkey."

When Jeff broke out on the border of the flowage he saw exactly what he had expected to see. There was

Gaston LaFleur, in his otter hat and striped mackinaw, diligently chiseling a hole in the ice a few rods from a beaver lodge.

Gaston's thick shoulders swung around at the sound of Jeff's approach. He looked startled; then, recognizing Jeff, a lazy smile worked over his face.

"So. My good fren', Jeff. How's the boy, eh?"

Jeff didn't return the smile. "I'm all right, Gaston. What are you doing here?"

Gaston's florid smile persisted. "Ice fishing may be. Thees a free countree, no?"

"And that, I suppose, is a fish pole." Jeff's hard eyes glanced at the spruce pole, freshly cut, that lay on the ice. It was ten feet long and six inches through.

Gaston's eyes narrowed. He still smiled but the smile was no longer amiable. "What's thees to you, eh? Gaston he cuts kind of fish pole he likes. You go run away."

Skip had come up now, taking in the situation with a quick eye. "Hey, this fellow's poaching. He's not supposed to be making preparation for beaver trapping until the deadline."

Gaston's chisel was fitted into an eight-foot pole. He took it up, holding it threateningly. His little black eyes were menacing. "You don' talk thees way to Gaston LaFleur!"

Jeff and Skip held their ground. Jeff said, and his voice

was quiet and steady: "We're staying right here. You're the one who's going to move."

Anger flamed on Gaston's face. Chisel raised, he moved towards them. He stopped quite suddenly. Jeff's hands balled into fists at his sides. The smile returned magically to Gaston's face.

"Gaston make a little joke, eh? You some feller. Thees a big countree. Plenty fur for everybody, eh?"

Jeff's hands relaxed, but his eyes were still cold. "We're greenhorns, Gaston, but we'll take our chances. All we want is an even chance."

"Sure thing," Gaston agreed happily. Then he beamed. "We're partners, eh? This a fine idea. You use my camp. I use your camp. We cover whole countree. Get plenty beaver. We divide up, eh? Half me, half you. Thees a fine idea."

"What about me?" Skip intervened. "There's three of us. If there's any partnership, we divvy three ways."

Gaston appealed to Jeff. "But he so little."

Gaston retreated as Skip flared up. "But ver' smart, eh," he added quickly. "Sure things."

Jeff's eyes didn't move from the Frenchman's. "We have a few other things to talk over, Gaston."

"Sure things," Gaston agreed cheerfully. He extended his big hand. "Now we partner, eh?"

"If it's all right with Skip, it's all right with me."

Skip hesitated. Before he could open his mouth, Jeff said: "He agrees. We're partners, Gaston, three ways. Come to our camp tomorrow. We'll lay out a plan."

Jeff was across the flowage and into the woods before Skip overtook him.

"Wait a minute! I didn't agree to anything. Don't you realize that he may be a — "

"Killer?" Jeff finished without breaking his stride. "He may be at that. If he is, we've got a better chance to watch him this way. If he isn't, we can use a friend. At least that's the way I figure it."

"Something tells me," Skip said uneasily, "that somebody's making a big mistake."

15. The Trap Line

The temperature was well below zero and still falling early the following evening when Gaston made his appearance at the camp. He left his snowshoes in the shed entry and came swaggering into the main room, his hairy hands cupped over his ears.

"*Nom de chien,* she col' like blue blazes, eh! Tomorrow we run a line. Gaston he show you how to get plenty beaver."

"Tomorrow at twelve o'clock noon," Jeff said pointedly. "That's how the law reads."

Gaston slapped the snow off his otter hat. He looked injured. "You think Gaston he don' know the law?"

"I guess you *know* the law all right, Gaston," Jeff laughed. "We're fixing up a rabbit stew. Will you eat with us?"

Gaston ambled over and sniffed at the concoction Skip was seasoning on the stove. "Sure things," Gaston agreed. "I make some biscuit, hey? Gaston's biscuit taste like something, I tell you!"

Without further words, Jeff produced the ingredients

and a piece of sheet iron. Gaston stripped off several layers of clothes and went to work.

After they had finished the meal and exchanged compliments on the cooking, the trio sat down and laid out a plan for covering the territory. It was decided that Skip would work with Gaston the first few days, running a line from across the lake south and east to Bog Stream. Jeff, working alone, would take north and west along the stream to Black, covering the ground he had cruised. They would utilize, when necessary, the other's home and line camps.

Gaston was pointing out one of his line camps that was situated on Bog Stream just below Black Lake.

Jeff remarked, reflectively: "That's near Willy Whiskers's cabin, isn't it? I thought I might drop by and say hello one of these days."

A dark shadow fell over Gaston's ruddy face. He tapped his head significantly. "Best things may be you stay away from this fellow."

"What do you know about him, Gaston?" Skip pressed.

Gaston's eyes were wary. "May be he crazy in the head. May be he not so crazy."

The boys exchanged glances. Jeff said in a careless voice, "What about this wolf, Gaston, this *loup-garou* you told me about?"

Gaston appeared puzzled for an instant. Then his good

spirits returned in full flood. He slapped his knee and chuckled. "You believe that, eh? Maybe Gaston make a good joke, no?"

"You mean to say," Skip said indignantly, "you were just trying to scare Jeff out of coming into this fur pocket? You said you heard a wolf in here."

Gaston grinned slyly. "May be. May be. May be I hear Gaston. Look, I show you."

He led the boys out into the bitter night. A few dim stars stippled the dark sky. The snow was a sweep of ghostly white across the lake.

Still grinning, Gaston arched back his bull neck and cupped his hands over his mouth. A wild primal cry issued from his lips and went quavering out across the night.

Jeff opened his mouth to speak as the cry died. His mouth remained open. From out of the black night the cry came back to them. Once, twice, the savage cry shattered the stillness; then silence again.

A cold chill worked up Jeff's back crawling into his hair. Beside him Skip gulped. Gaston's face looked white as the snow. His arm hung stiffly at his side.

"Echo," Gaston said irresolutely. Then he nodded his head with conviction. "By dam' me, you hear Gaston's echo?"

"Echo, my eye!" Jeff whispered. "You only called once."

"Not everybody can make double echo," Gaston

snapped. He wheeled and hurried back into the cabin, the boys at his heels.

Jeff slept with one eye open that night, but the night cry was not repeated. The only sound he heard was the growl of the lake ice expanding, punctuated at intervals by sharp reports like a ricocheting bullet, as the deepening ice reefed on the lake.

It was quite obvious that Gaston hadn't slept too well that night. He was shaken and uncommunicative. It was in silence that they packed their traps and gear, and prepared to set out on the big day.

The traps were packed in pack baskets along with wire, staples, a pair of wire-cutting pliers and an ice chisel. They each carried a cold lunch, a waterproof match case, a compass and hand ax.

They were getting into snowshoes in the clearing when Gaston spoke. "We run the trap line. We meet here two day, yes? Gaston stay here with you boys. You need company, eh?"

"We've got company, Skip and I," Jeff said. "But it's all right with us, I guess."

"You need company," Gaston insisted sharply.

The boys' glances brushed, momentarily. Skip's shoulders hunched in a small inconclusive shrug. "Right," Jeff said. With a wave of his hand he pushed off westward, alone.

It was the hardest day's work Jeff White had ever put in, in his life. He worked all the way to Black Lake, making beaver sets. There were holes to cut in the ice, poles to cut and poplar bait to cut. Placing the traps on the chair, hands and arms in the icy water with a numbing wind blowing across the flowages, was something less than a picnic.

He reached his Black Lake camp just before dark, his hands sore and bleeding from wire handling, his feet numb from cold — too exhausted to feel hunger.

But he knew he must eat. He built a fire in the drum stove and rammed some snow in the kettle to make water for tea. His hands began to ache as the warmth took hold. With a handful of snow he massaged the blood back into them. He ate what he had in his pack. A cold rabbit joint, some hard biscuits and a handful of raisins.

He stoked the fire solid with green wood, banked up ashes against the draft door, and burrowing into the bedroll went to sleep as though he had been rapped on the head with a mallet.

When he awoke before dawn the wind was still blowing. Jeff rose, flexed his muscles back into life and opened up the fire. The moon was just going down when he finished his tea and the remaining biscuits. There was enough light to work, he decided. He put out the fire, slung his pack basket on his back, and hit the trail.

His plan was to cruise up Bog Stream, make a few more sets if he found a likely location, and then swing west, checking the upper reaches of some of the tributary brooks. From there he would circle back over the mountain and inspect the cat traps on the way into the home camp. Skip had promised to check the cat traps the day before on his swing, for the law read that, with the exception of beaver sets, all traps must be patrolled every twenty-four hours.

It was going to be warmer that day and almost windless, Jeff decided. It would be a fine day. None the less, Jeff's thoughts were disquieting. What was wrong with Gaston? Was Gaston really frightened? Or was he just pretending to be frightened? That was a very important question. If he was truly scared, what was he scared about? If he was pretending to be frightened — well, what was the point?

And Gaston had known Blackie Barron — of this Jeff was convinced. Jeff also guessed that Gaston had hated Blackie. That didn't mean necessarily that Gaston had killed him; most people who knew Blackie had hated him. In fact, there was no real proof that Blackie's death had been anything but accidental. But who had removed the body, and why? Jeff was pretty sure that even Jack Bailey was unsatisfied with the bear theory. There was no sense in bringing Old Carrie's disappearance into the muddle. There was probably no connection at all.

"And what's more," Jeff said aloud, "I'm in here to trap."

Then Jeff's thoughts came back to earth with a jolt. He'd been seeing the tracks for some moments. They just hadn't registered. Running just abreast of him were a set of prints made within the hour by bear-paw type snow-shoes.

Those were bear-paw snowshoe tracks that had come into their camp that afternoon! That didn't mean much, Jeff told himself, holding back the hot rush of excitement in his chest. That type of snowshoe wasn't uncommon. He was near Willy's camp. Those, undoubtedly, were Willy's tracks.

And Willy was a friend. Hadn't Buck assured him that Willy Whiskers could be counted on as a friend?

Jeff had not been aware of coming to any decision; but there he was going straight out on the trail. He had said he wanted to say hello to Willy. Well, he'd say hello.

It was twenty minutes later that he came upon the sod hut, unexpectedly. The hut was wide, low-eaved and so completely covered with snow that it appeared to be part of the forest. What betrayed its presence was a chopping block in the small clearing, and the single window to the right of the doorway. Yes, and the tiny spiral of wood smoke curling from the stone chimney.

No sound came from the dwelling. Jeff moved cautiously across the clearing. The door was crude with wooden hand-whittled latch and hinges.

No answer came to his soft rap. He knocked again and then called: "Willy, it's Jeff. Jeff White. You remember me. I'm a friend of Warden Larrabee."

There was still no answer. And no sound of movement. He tried the door gently. It was fastened tight — from within.

Jeff was aware of a strange uneasiness. He moved over to press his face against the window. A ragged piece of burlap sacking blocked his vision.

He was standing there, irresolutely, when he saw the mound of earth at the edge of the clearing. There in the center of a tangled patch of wild raspberry bushes was a heap of dirt shaped, for all the world, like a grave.

He strode over to the brier thicket and pushed in a few feet. Why, it was a grave! A cedar spit served as a marker and on it was scrawled in black crayon:

MY DOG HUNTER
A TRUE AND LOYAL FRIEND

So Willy's faithful dog was dead! Perhaps that explained Willy's strange conduct. Perhaps he was mourning or, more likely, was afraid without the protection of his guardian dog. But, after all, was there any reason to believe that this furtiveness was strange conduct for Willy? Willy was admittedly strange.

Well, strange or not, Jeff decided, there was nothing much he could do if the wilderness hermit wanted to be left strictly alone. With one last glance at the hut, Jeff started on the back trail home.

It was when he turned once again at the wood's edge that he thought he saw movement at the window. There was nothing there now. Nothing at all. But he was almost certain that he had seen, for a brief instant, the be-whiskered face of Willy Whiskers staring out at him.

It was an hour before dark when Jeff, crossing over the mountain, reached his first cat set. In that one there was a prize — a snarling young cat which he dispatched. He reset the trap and pushed on. There was nothing else until he came to his last set on that string. There he found a prime red fox. He killed him quickly. He didn't wait to rough-skin on the trail. He tossed the fox into his pack basket. He wanted to be in before dark, and night was almost upon him.

He was pushing down the trail on the last mile from the lake when he heard the drone of a plane. He couldn't see it for the thick growth, but he recognized the engine of the warden's Piper Cruiser. Smoky was coming in.

Jeff opened up his stride on the broken trail and struck for camp.

16. News from Home

WILL HIBBS and Buck Larrabee were standing around the stove with the warden pilot, drinking hot tea, when Jeff came in through the shed.

The wardens greeted him warmly. Will clapped him on the back. "You look healthy and thriving, Tracker. How's everything going?"

"I've just put in a rugged two days on the trail," Jeff told him as he slipped out of his pack. "All I've got to show for it yet is a cat and a fox. What brings you in?"

"We've had a couple of rugged days ourselves," Buck tossed in. "We've been checking trappers and trap lines all the way to the border, Will and I. With a little help from Smoky here, of course."

"A *little* help!" Smoky snorted. "How would you like to cruise that territory we've covered, on foot? Say, where's your partner, Jeff?"

"He should be in by now," Jeff said a little anxiously. "He's swinging a circle with Gaston."

The men looked at one another. Jeff explained briefly

their arrangement with the Frenchman. "We decided it was better to have him with us than against us."

"The fact is," Will said slowly, "we figured to check Gaston and see how many trapping laws he's broken so far. And Jack wanted us to ask him a few questions about Blackie Barron."

"Then Gaston did know Blackie?"

"He knew him all right," Warden Larrabee said. He stripped a stick of gum and plopped it into his mouth. "We got a violation report on Blackie from Augusta. He and Gaston were partners some years back and were caught together with a pack of poached beaver in the Allagash Country. Gaston wasn't a citizen then. We turned him over to the Border Patrol on illegal entry.

"A year later they were back at it. At least Blackie came out of the woods that spring with his arm laid open from the wrist to his shoulder. It took fifty stitches to sew him up. He said he was going to kill Gaston on sight when he met up with him again. I guess the prison doors closed on him before he could catch up to Gaston."

Will sat down on the bunk and took out his pipe. "Jack was hoping you boys might have run onto that body in your travels."

Jeff shook his head. "And I'm not unhappy about that; finding him once was enough for me!"

"And that's not all we found out about that pretty character," Will added. "Parker West took enough time off from rabbit hunting to run up to Portage where Blackie was brought up. He couldn't get along with his family, particularly his brother, who was a little odd and kept bringing home stray dogs. Blackie hated animals. One day, he kicked his brother's dog once too often, and his brother went for him with an ax and almost killed him. A few days after that his brother disappeared and was never seen or heard from again. Some people up there still think Blackie murdered his brother, but nothing was ever proved!"

Jeff shook his head. "Holy ole mackinaw! Another missing body! That's three of them that haven't been found."

"You can take Carrie off the list," Will put in. "She was found the day Skip came in."

"Alive?"

Will smiled. "Alive and kicking. It takes more than a crack on the noggin to do in Old Carrie. She couldn't help us much," Will added soberly. "She heard a sound outside and left her supper to investigate. She had a glimpse of a figure heading towards the woods. Carrie, being Carrie, lit right out after him. Whoever it was waited and waylaid her. I expect he left her for dead. Carrie must have wandered in the woods several days not knowing who she was or where she was going. A farmer, over Bolton way, found her still traveling and took her in. It was days more before the farmer finally got to town one day and learned of the hunt for a missing woman."

Jeff whistled. "What a woman! Then you don't think there's any connection . . . ?"

"You mean between Carrie's bump on the head and the body of Blackie Barron. Well, hardly. Buck here isn't convinced, though. He asked Carrie what she was uneasy about when she sent that note to Willy. She was indignant. It was Willy she was uneasy about. On his last trip he'd told her someone was trailing him. She insists it's Willy who needs protection, not she. But what Willy's got that anyone could want, is more than I can see."

"I'd say," Jeff replied, "that he sure has a case of jitters." He quickly recounted his visit and his discovery of Hunter's grave. "I'm sure I saw Willy's face at the window."

The wardens looked at one another. Will said: "Maybe one of us ought to look in on Willy, Buck."

"Let's get this thing settled." Smoky was checking his watch. "I've got to hop out of here before dark."

"It's settled," Buck said, "I'm staying in, Will. This is my district, and I should do a bit of cruising through here anyway." He tossed a grin at the warden pilot. "Just don't forget I'm here, brother. Pick me up in a few days."

Smoky tied on his parka. "Right. Got any reports for Chuck?"

"Tell him I'll report when I see him."

Will was getting his big frame into his red winter jacket. He frowned. "Are you worried about Skipper? You said he was due in."

"I'm not really worried. It wasn't too definite when he'd be in. They might have hung over in Gaston's camp for the night. They'd be swinging back that way."

Will's blue eyes were still thoughtful. "I don't know how far you should trust Gaston, Tracker."

"I don't either," Jeff admitted. "We'll keep our eyes open."

"You do that. And happy trapping."

There was handshaking all around at the doorway. Buck at his side, Jeff waved Will and the pilot to the plane. A few moments later the plane roared to life. They both gave a final wave as the plane skidded across the sweep of the lake and slanted upward into the darkening sky.

Buck's chewing jaws revolved slowly as he moved back into the warm camp. "I don't get it. Willy's met you. What's he afraid of? I hope he hasn't started hearing wolves too." Then he shrugged off the frown. "You start and build a supper while I show you how to skin out that fur you fetched in; and let's have some pleasant conversation."

It was dark when they finished supper that night. Buck had skun out the cat and fox, and Jeff set to fleshing the pelts.

"I'd tack up your green pelts in the shed if I were you," Buck suggested. "You can ruin a good fur, you know, drying it too near a fire. How many beaver are you counting on tomorrow?"

"I'm not counting on any. And I'd be pleased to find one or two."

Buck saw the excitement in the boy's face. He grinned. "Quite a game, eh, Jeff? And don't think a trapper ever gets over feeling the way you do now. The excitement never gets out of their blood once they're bit. It's like a poker gambler. He's always wondering what's going to be in his next hand right up to the day he dies. Old toe-pinchers have told me that some nights they just can't sleep wondering what they're going to find in their traps the next day. It's like a drug, boy. And when you're once bit, you're bit for life."

"I am wondering," Jeff admitted, "but I guess I can sleep all right. I'd better. I've got twenty miles to cover tomorrow."

They were preparing to turn in when they heard the steps at the door. The door was swung open, and Skip Doggett, looking pale and stiff with cold, pushed into the camp.

"Skip!" Jeff greeted him. "It's sure good to see you in! What held you up? Where's Gaston?"

It was some moments before Skip could speak. He inched off his ice-rimmed mittens, shrugged out of his parka. "I guess you might say that I'm lucky to be here. I don't think I would have got my bearings back if I hadn't seen that plane take off."

"Where's Gaston?" Jeff pressed him. "I thought he was coming back with you?"

"He was, but he didn't. Gaston's going out."

"Going out?"

"We came across a track this afternoon near Goose Brook. Something happened to Gaston when he saw that track."

Buck was on his feet now. "What kind of a track?"

Skip shook his head. "Gaston didn't say. It looked like whatever it was had been inspecting a deer carcass. Gaston didn't say much at all. It was the way he looked."

"He just went off and left you?"

"All he said was 'By crize, I think I go now,' and he went."

Buck reached for his pack of gum. "This thing," Buck remarked, "is getting crazier and crazier."

17. Another Grisly Discovery

It was two days later that Jeff caught his first beaver. Coming upon his first set two miles north of the home camp, he knelt and pushed away the slushed snow from his ice hole and saw the dark glossy shape below. Heart pounding wildly, he bent closer to be sure, shielding the glare with his body.

There was no mistake about it. As in all water sets, the animal had died quickly and humanely. He worked quickly in the ice water. In a moment his first prize — a fat prime female — lay on the snow. Still unsteady from excitement, he rough-skinned the beaver on the spot, not wishing to carry the extra load on his circle.

It's a slow and tedious process to skin a beaver so that it will need no further fleshing. Since it is easy to score a beaver pelt when working close, Jeff used the professional method of cutting deep and skinning rough.

Jeff stowed the carcass in a tree with the idea of picking it up on the way back. It would make good cat bait. Also it would be a change in their own diet. The Indians considered the beaver flesh a delicacy. Jeff wasn't quite sure how Skip would feel about it, but personally he was anxious to give it a try.

There was no more booty in that particular pond. Working north and west on his circle that day, however, he was rewarded twice more. When he arrived at his line camp that night, he had in addition to his female, a yearling and a large blanket-size male.

He was back at the home camp late the following day, having picked up one more pelt on the back circle. Skip was there in high spirits.

"I fetched in three of them!" he announced. "And I'm not even a trapper. I wouldn't call it the easiest way to make a living, though."

"Say, we've practically made expenses already. This won't keep up. We'll probably go a week now without a smell of fur."

"Stop it," Skip pleaded; "let's pretend we don't know any better. Hey, supper's on. You're going to be surprised."

Jeff had noted the delicious odor issuing from the oven. He sniffed again; then looked quizzically at his young partner. "It smells like roast pork, but it couldn't be."

"That's right," Skip said grinning, "it couldn't be. But it could be roast beaver tail."

"Then you *do* want to try it?"

"Sure. After you," Skip said. "I cooked it the way we used to when I was a boy trapper on the Allagash. I impaled it on a green stick and blistered off the skin by holding it over the open fire. Now I'll roast it until tender. In those days, of course, we didn't have ovens — "

"But we sure have," Jeff said wearily, "just as many fancy liars."

The roasted white-meated flesh of the beaver tail looked delicious and what was most important it tasted rich and sustaining. Warden Larrabee came stomping in as they were about to take second helpings.

"Take it easy, boys," he exhorted. "If that's beaver tail, you've got a ravenous guest. A man doesn't get a treat like that every day in the week."

There was plenty for all, and the fact that the rice that garnished the meat wasn't quite cooked didn't deter any one of them from cleaning the platter.

They were washing down the meal with hot tea when Buck, loosening his belt, began relating his experiences of the past two days.

"First off, I might tell you that Gaston didn't go out. I picked up his tracks and he was heading north and east. He went as far as Willy Whiskers's camp but he didn't go into it. Judging from his tracks, he stood watching Willy's camp for some time. I had the same luck you had, Jeff. Willy just isn't interested in visitors."

"What about Gaston?" Skip wanted to know. "Did you follow him?"

Buck nodded. "I thought at first he was on a trap line. But he wasn't. What he was on were some old snowshoe tracks. Willy's, I'd guess. They were three or four days old, so it didn't make any sense. Not to me, anyhow. When Gaston started to swing south for home, I gave up. I still give up."

Buck rose and plopped a stick of gum in his mouth. "Boys, I've got some trap lines and camps to check out beyond Hatchet Mountain. I'll be gone anywhere from two days to a week. I'm striking out at dawn if you think you'll be all right."

"Don't worry about us," Jeff assured him. "What if the warden pilot shows up for you?"

"Tell Smoky to cruise over Lowden Pond. If he sees a green-brush fire he can set down there and pick me up. If not, he can pick me up here on his next trip in."

Skip was looking very solemn. "You know," he said, "I've got a hunch that Gaston knows something."

Buck frowned. "If you mean about that body he doesn't have to know much to know more than I do."

In the morning Buck was gone. The boys spent a few days on their trap lines without a single reward. They took turns swinging back and checking the cat traps.

These mountain sets produced one fox and another cat which were gratefully accepted.

The fourth day after Buck's departure was so bitter cold that the air seemed to lacerate their lungs. They both stayed close to camp that day replenishing their fuel supply and practicing Gaston's wolf call with the idea of using it as a contact signal in the woods.

They had no word nor saw any sign of Gaston LaFleur. Both boys, though neither spoke of it, were aware of a rising tension within them. It was as though they were waiting for something to happen and not knowing what to expect.

The weather moderated the following day. And that day their bad luck on the trap line broke. Jeff turned up in camp with three fat beaver, and Skip was there to greet him with one blanket beaver and two yearlings.

They celebrated that night with another feast of roast beaver tail. Before turning in that night they lay on their bunks listening to the wind. It was Skip who spoke first.

"You haven't mentioned those fisher again. I've been seeing quite a few tracks."

"I've been thinking about them, too," Jeff admitted. "I've been thinking we ought to leave them alone. You can't eat a fisher, and long-haired fur isn't worth much these days. The way I figure it is this. If we leave them alone, they'll be here. And when the fisher price comes back, we can always come in."

"I guess you're right," Skip agreed with some reluctance. "I just thought it might be fun to track one down on snowshoes."

It was some moments before Jeff spoke. "I guess what I mean is that trapping shouldn't be sport. You trap for a living or you trap for food. Take Gaston. He's a rascal all right, but he's a woodsman, too. I don't think even Gaston has ever trapped for fun."

"Let's take Gaston," Skip suggested. "He's not here for fun. He's not here for fun and he's not here for trapping. I've been staying awake nights trying to figure Gaston out."

Jeff yawned. "You stay awake and worry about Gaston. I'm going to get a hunk of sleep."

It was sometime in the middle of the night that Jeff was brought rudely from sleep by Skip's shout. "What's the matter with you?" he demanded, rubbing his eyes.

"I said 'I've got it.'"

"You've got what?"

"What Gaston's up to, of course. It just came to me."

"Can't you hold onto it until morning?"

"Maybe I can, but I'm not going to. Don't you see, Blackie came into the woods with all that money he stole. Blackie's dead. But the money's here."

"So?"

"So Gaston's looking for it. He thinks Willy's looking for it too. Or maybe he thinks Willy either has it or knows where it's hidden. That's why he was following his tracks."

Jeff was fully awake now. He felt his head, shook it a little. "In the middle of the night it takes time for a brilliant idea like that to soak in. Maybe you're right."

"You bet I'm right! I didn't take that mail-order course in criminal detection for nothing. It's a hot lead and we're going to follow it up."

"You took the course, I didn't," Jeff said. "How do we follow it up?"

"It's all there in my book. We get into his camp under false pretenses. Let's see now, we couldn't be checking his electric light meter or selling magazines — "

"Couldn't we," Jeff offered, "just make a friendly visit?"

"Watson, you're wonderful," Skip trumpeted. "Why didn't I think of that? After all we're friends — or are we?"

"Maybe," Jeff said. "We'll find out."

There was a feel of coming snow in the air as they set out across the lake at dawn that next morning. The low overcast seemed to press down upon the treetops. The air was so still it was ominous.

There was no smoke issuing from the small camp of

Gaston LaFleur as the boys came into the clearing. The log house, with its roof of rough cedar splits, seemed strangely silent. Jeff stepped ahead and rapped on the door. Hearing no sound, he called Gaston's name.

"I think we ought to go in," Skip said. "Gaston did say we were welcome to use his camp."

Jeff already had the rude latch in his hand and was pressing against the door with his shoulder. The door gave way. Jeff took three steps into the room. He stopped as though he'd come to the brink of a precipice.

Behind him, Skip's breath hissed sharply. "It's Gaston. He — he's dead!"

There on the rough board floor he lay face down, one clenched hand stretched forward. He wore his woolen pants but no outer shirt. A stain of blood, brown and dry, showed on his gray underwear just below the shoulder blade.

Jeff saw the thing in his hand. He reached down and took the .22 bullet from the stiff fingers. And crouching there beside him, he saw what had been Gaston LaFleur's last act on earth.

On the rough floor he had written something with the lead end of the cartridge. Skip, now down on his hands and knees, read it aloud.

It not Willy who knifed me it . . .

It was then that Gaston had died.

Both boys were on their feet now, facing one another. Skip's lips moved, feebly. "If Willy didn't kill him, then who did? Who — who else is there?"

Young Jeff's eyes were arctic. "I think," he said, "we'd better try and find out."

18. Night Vigil

A CHANGE seemed to come over Jeff White as he stood here in that room with death. A boy doesn't become a man in a glimmering. There is a twilight stage when he is neither one nor the other but a mixture of both. In that moment the man took control in Jeff White.

Jeff said: "We're right in the middle of something, Skipper. We've got to think. We've got to think fast and think right."

Skip had yanked a dark wool blanket from the bunk. He laid it over the prone body. "First let's cover this up. Seeing Gaston like that sort of interferes with my thinking. What do you think we ought to do?"

Jeff's eyes reached over the room. The place was a shambles. "It looks as though Gaston died fighting. I guess we can guess why he was killed."

Skipper snapped his fingers. "The money! He stumbled on the hiding place. If Gaston figured it out, we ought to be able to."

"The wolf," Jeff whispered, "that wolf's got to figure in

it somehow. It was the wolf that must have given Gaston his final clue. We've got to find that wolf, Skip!"

"Are you crazy," Skip protested. "What could a wolf know? And say he does know something. And say you do want to get close enough to a wolf to have a powwow. Are you going to learn wolf, or teach the wolf English? What we ought to do is set a green-brush fire and signal for help."

"We can't expect help until we get some flying weather. We can't even expect help from Warden Larrabee until after the storm. He's holed up some place. But there is someone we ought to contact."

"Willy Whiskers!" Skip nodded resolutely. "Gaston must have learned something from Willy. If Willy knows something, then he's in danger too. But what I want to do first of all is get out of this place."

Skip was standing near the window. "Golly diamonds! Hey, look at this! We're going to be lucky if we find the lake in this!"

One quick glance was all Jeff needed to confirm Skip's dire opinion of their plight. A roaring, swirling snowstorm was funneling out of the north. The snow was falling so thickly he could just barely perceive the trees looming beyond the clearing. Already their own snowshoe tracks had been obliterated.

There was authority in Jeff's voice as he spoke: "We're

going to try it. We've got to get back. I don't think we've got much time and we've got to be ready."

Skip's eyes narrowed. "Wait a minute," he said uneasily, "much time for what? What do you expect is going to happen?"

Tight-lipped, Jeff said: "If someone knows as much as I think he does about our movements, I think we can expect a visitor."

Skip winced. "And we want to wait? I'm not sure I like the smell of this. It doesn't say a thing in my book about a detective acting as bait for a killer."

"We haven't much choice, have we?" Jeff asked quietly. "And if we've got to wait, I can't think of a better place than our own camp. Besides, our guns are there. I don't think we're in danger until the killer is convinced we do know something."

"If that's the case," Skip said, "I've even forgotten the name of the first President of the United States. And don't tell me!"

They made the crossing with the wind full in their faces. Jeff had taken a compass bearing, and, compass in his mittened hand, they breasted the storm. It seemed that they had been traveling hours on the open lake before Jeff's straining eyes found the shape of trees ahead.

With Skip close behind him, he pushed into the thicket. The snow fell even more thickly now and the wind made a sea roar in the trees. He moved ahead like a blind man, hand outthrust, his chin pressed down against his chest to protect his numb face from the icy blast.

The camp is to the south, he told himself. This is near where that ledge comes out over to the water. Fear took hold of him and shook him. For he knew he wasn't sure. Stick to the lake — that was the thing to do. His hand caught hold of a low hanging fir branch and he eased himself up over a blowdown.

He stopped and a great welling of relief filled his chest. There were fresh cut stumbles on that tree. This was where they had cut their last load of fire boughs for bedding. The camp was just fifty yards along the lake to the left.

"Come on!" Jeff shouted above the primal voice of the storm. "We're home!"

A few moments later they were in their camp with a crackling fire going. They both stripped down to their underwear and hung their wet, iced clothes near the warmth. They had their dinner cooked and half eaten before either boy said a word.

Jeff was checking the cylinder of his handgun. "I said we were in no danger until we figured this thing out. I've got a hunch the answer is as plain as the nose on your face. In one way it might be better if we did know the answer. Then we might know who to expect. Any ideas, Inspector?"

"My mind's a perfect blank," Skip assured him. He smiled weakly. "Don't misunderstand me. I don't mind being tortured a little. Why, I remember the time I was captured by some cannibals — "

"There's not enough fat on you to interest any cannibals," Jeff snorted. "Okay, let's get some sleep while we have a chance. I don't think we'll have any callers until this storm lets up. We'll both wake up with a fresh mind."

"If we wake up at all," Skip remarked darkly.

They turned in that night with the wind roaring in their ears. The snow lashed the windowpane, and the driving wind rattled at the tightly latched door as though demanding entry.

Jeff dozed off to sleep that night wondering about more things than his mind could contain. He must have slept, for suddenly he was awake and bolt upright in his bunk. He listened. He had heard that wild, elemental cry of a wolf. Now there was only the wild cry of the wind.

He had been dreaming, that was it. He fell back into an uneasy sleep convinced that this was so.

The storm had abated somewhat by morning. In the gray light of dawn when they crawled from their bunks, they could see the sky. But the snow still came down. The snow had drifted to the level of the window.

They had their breakfast without much talk. When the dishes were cleaned up, Jeff's restlessness didn't subside.

Who was this killer? What were they waiting for? Was it someone they knew? Was it someone they would receive as a friend?

Skip's eyes were on him. Skip said: "You didn't hear that wolf last night, did you? I had a dream — "

"You heard it?" Jeff had stopped in the center of the room. Then he shook his head roughly. "It's nerves. That's what it is. You couldn't hear a wolf above that wind unless he was at our doorstep."

Skip shuddered. "Do you think that makes it any better? A wolf at our door, no less."

Suddenly Jeff reached for his boots. "Look," he said, "I'm stepping out for a few moments. I'm just going to make a short swing. I'll be right back."

Skip, who was slouched at the table, sat up. "What are you up to?"

Jeff shrugged. "I don't know. I just want to look around."

He hauled on his boots, slid into an extra shirt and drew on his parka. He reached for the handgun that lay on his bunk. "I'll take this in case I see a rabbit."

Skip didn't stir, but he met Jeff's eyes head on. "And in case I see a killer, what would you suggest?"

Jeff said, "You've got that .30-30. If I were you, I'd put a few rounds in the magazine."

19. The Stalk

ALTHOUGH wind-torn clouds still marched across the sweep of sky, the snow had stopped falling. The storm appeared to have blown itself out. Jeff had no clear-cut plan in his mind as he struck out on snowshoes across the fresh snow. It was just that sitting and waiting for something to happen was intolerable.

There was a killer at large. If he had murdered two people and stunned Carrie — and Jeff was convinced now that all three incidents were connected — he wouldn't hesitate to kill again. If he was going to strike, it would be now during the storm's lull.

His snowshoes made no sound for the new snow was as soft as down. He moved as slowly as a stalking cat, all his senses keyed to pin-point alertness.

"If he is here," Jeff told himself, "I've got to see him before he sees me."

That was the stalker's challenge. The white hunter had learned the primitive art from the Indian. The Indian had learned from the wildcat, the fox, the weasel.

Jeff had stalked deer, but it had been without fear for himself. Now, as he moved, he knew fear; and knowing it, he felt for the first time in his life not an invader of the wilderness, but a part of it.

Take the deer or the robin. They must learn fear; it is not bred into them. The bird doesn't leave the nest or the deer his mother until he recognizes danger and is equipped to cope with it.

Jeff knew fear as he slowly circled the camp. But he was aware of it in a way that a deer or a rabbit is incapable of knowing it. A rabbit nibbling at the dew-drenched grass, although he has a deep-knowing fear that protects him, has no knowledge of death. He cannot imagine death, for he cannot reflect upon himself. The stalking weasel strikes. His throat is torn. He is dead. The rabbit's death from the weasel's onslaught is mercifully brief, his knowledge of terror as short-lived as the wink of an eye.

But Jeff moved that day with a fear no animal can ever know — the fear of death.

And now, just north of the camp, he stopped and froze into immobility. Nothing moved in the woods; the only sound was the sound that came from a tree full of foraging chickadees near by. Just ahead, canting to the west, was a trail of fresh snowshoe tracks.

It was a moment for decision. Jeff hesitated but an instant. He had told Skip he wouldn't go far, that he wouldn't be long. But if this were the killer, wouldn't it be better to know who he was and where he was than to return and wait for his coming, not knowing who or what to expect?

His decision made, Jeff took a quick compass bearing, checked the wind, and picked up the trail. He traveled even more cautiously now, stopping every few rods to look and listen. The track led along a hardwood ridge, and the wooded slope was free of thickets. But the going soon became rougher as the trail turned south across the snarled brier growth of an old burn.

"Is he swinging back towards the camp?" Jeff thought with a rush of panic. Perhaps he'd been a fool to take up this trail. All he could think to do was to increase his pace and try to close up the distance between them.

He stopped abruptly. Just to the left something had moved. Jeff spun around. But there was nothing stirring, nothing amiss. Maybe it was this inexplicable feeling he had, a feeling he couldn't shake off, that he was being watched. Or was it just that he was scared? When you're afraid, your fear feeds your imagination. You're apt to see all kinds of shapes and sounds.

He pushed on. He had to keep his fear under control. There was enough real danger lurking without multiplying it with fancies of his mind. But he wished the wind would stop whining so dolefully in the trees. It sounded like a human chorus. It sounded like church funeral music. . . .

Jeff thought: "If I only knew what to expect. If something strikes, will it be a singing bullet or the lunge of a wild beast?"

Then again, he came to an abrupt halt. Another track had crossed the man track he was following. He hadn't been mistaken! He had seen something! The large dog-like track that crossed the trail was so fresh the snow in its depressions was still settling!

He came sharply erect, his eyes ranging the woods. Nothing. There was no turning back now. Danger was all around him. There would be no freedom from danger now until he knew the truth. Ahead somewhere, he was sure, lay the answer.

He reached into his parka pocket and felt the small comforting shape of the handgun that nestled there. He went forward once more, his head now up, his eyes scouring the woods. He was poised to surmount an obstructing blowdown when, just to the right, a fugitive shape moved in the shadows of a thicket. Then, once again, there was nothing at all.

How long he stood there motionless, Jeff did not know. It was the creeping, penetrating cold that forced him to stir at last. His hands were numb, and the frigid air cut his lungs like shards of glass. Mechanically, he placed one shoe ahead of the other, circling the blowdown. Moving, stopping, moving again, he came up over a gentle rise of ground.

Just beyond was a clearing. The man tracks led into it and across it towards a tangled patch of wild raspberries. Then he knew where he was! Just beyond was Willy Whiskers's camp. And where those tracks led into the brier patch was the grave of Willy's dog, Hunter!

Had the killer come for Willy? Was it already too late to warn the wilderness recluse? Crouching low, Jeff moved in closer, using whatever scrap of cover he could find to screen his approach. The coming darkness favored him now. He achieved the edge of the clearing. He waited, listening, his eyes seeking he knew not what. Nothing happened. Nothing moved.

He could see now where the man had shed his snow-shoes so they wouldn't encumber his passage through the brier maze. His tracks crossed the grave and broke through the other side of the patch. There he had slipped into his snowshoes again and traveled on.

And what was that on the grave? It was something red. A bandana, or a mitten. The killer — if this was the killer — had dropped it! It would be a clue to his identity. At least it must be some kind of a clue! He knew then he had to follow that trail across the grave.

He took but one step forward. His muscles stiffened.

A chill raked his back. There had been no sound at all, but there, fifty feet off at the other edge of the clearing, the shape was clearly defined. He wasn't seeing a fancy now! In the dusk, in the deepening owl-light, two yellow eyes seemed to be regarding him with enormous, unblinking calm.

Even as he recoiled, reaching for his gun, the great dog-like shape sprang forward. He was hurtling across the clearing, a dark running form as soundless as the falling snow. Jeff fell backwards, struggling to free his gun. In that awful instant he closed his eyes, expecting the assault of tearing fangs.

What he heard instead was a blood-chilling animal cry of pain and hate.

The great animal had come down the track of the killer straight into the brier patch. That was the trail he himself would have followed in another moment — followed to his destruction! For there the wolf lay, writhing, struggling in a fruitless frenzy to free himself from the cruel jaws of a forty-pound bear trap!

Wolf? The truth came bludgeoning home! This "wolf" wore a collar! This wasn't a wolf at all! It was a large wolflike dog. Of course! It was Willy's dog. It was Willy's Malemute, Hunter!

Then the revelation flashed upon his brain. Hunter and Willy were inseparable. If Hunter was running wild that meant — of course! Hadn't he told Skip that the answer must be as plain as the nose on his face?

And if Hunter wasn't buried in that grave then what was buried there? What indeed! It was clear now that Gaston had died because he had ferreted out the secret.

It not Willy who knifed me, Gaston had scrawled. Of course it wasn't Willy! And the razor! Horror overwhelmed him as the grim use to which that razor had been put struck him.

Fear came larruping back. The door of the camp had opened. It was still swinging back slowly. In the dim light of the thickening dusk, he saw the shape of a rifle barrel. Instinctively, Jeff sought his own gun. It was gone! He had dropped it somewhere in the snow when the dog had sprung.

Then the gun flashed. The dog on the grave quivered once, then lay still.

"You devil dog," a low grating voice said. "So it was you on my trail! I expected another prize, but you'll do."

The dark, towering shape was moving across the clearing, rifle cradled in his arms. His whiskered face was in shadow, but Jeff, crouching low in the screening thicket, knew fear was written there.

And there was fear in that voice as the man hesitated at the edge of the briers. "I thought I'd killed you once. I thought I'd been hearing things at night. There'll be no more howling at night, now! You're dead now. And you'll stay dead."

Jeff crouched lower as the great hulking figure pushed through the briers to the grave. He had a pair of turn-screw clamps in his hands. He set down his gun, kicked the inert form once, and bent over to screw down the trap springs and open the steel jaws of the bear trap.

Jeff was already easing his body backwards. He knew what he had to do. He had to get away. He had to get back for help. Unarmed, he could do nothing. The killer would not escape so long as he felt safe behind those whiskers. Back at camp he and Skip would build the biggest green-brush fire they could rustle up. They needed to signal for help now. They needed to get that warden plane in!

The black figure was intent on resetting the trap now. Jeff got his feet under him. He froze as the whiskered face came up. The man had the trap set and was dusting it over with snow. Perhaps he should wait now until the man had gone back into the camp. But what if the killer made a circle and saw his tracks?

Jeff reached for the support of an overhanging fir branch. It gave under his weight with a loud crack. He was down on his back in the snow when he saw the dark shape rise up from the grave. Jeff felt a rush of panic possess him. Momentarily, his impulse was to scramble to his feet and make a dash for it. That was his only chance now. He was sure of it.

The figure had stepped toward him. He was peering into the shadows. Jeff lay motionless. The black figure stood barely fifty feet away. There was fear in the set of those shoulders. This ruthless killer was afraid! In that long and terrifying moment, Jeff knew that he had one weapon left.

Cautiously, noiselessly, Jeff inched away — ten feet — twenty feet. He stripped his mittens from his hands. He and Skip had practiced Gaston's wolf call. Now that his life depended on it, he wished he had practiced more. If he could use fear to immobilize this man for a few precious moments, it might give him time to get away. This *had* to be right!

He laid back his head. He cupped his bare hands over his mouth and sucked breath deep into his lungs. From his throat came the sound, a wild quavering cry that reached high into the treetops. It was the elemental howl of a hunting wolf.

He saw the shape of the man stiffen. Jeff sent out the cry once more. Guttural sounds came from the man on the grave. Through the trees he saw the figure recoil, step back. A rending cry of pain shattered the stillness. He had sprung the trap! The black figure fell clawing at the snow, his booted foot caught fast in steel jaws.

178

Jeff was on his feet when he heard, far off to the east-ward, an answering cry. The thrust of terror dissolved in a prayer. He knew what that cry meant. It was Skipper Doggett answering. Skipper was on his way!

He was waiting at the edge of the clearing when he saw two figures coming towards him through the woods. The sky had cleared, and in the light of a fragmentary moon he discerned the square shape of Buck Larrabee; behind him came Skipper Doggett.

Skip gave forth with a shout as he spied Jeff. "We were on our way when I heard your wolf call," Skip said as he came up. "You gave me the scare of my life! I thought sure you'd run into some kind of trouble."

Buck's hand was on Jeff's shoulder. The warden's face looked gray and strained. "I shouldn't have left you boys alone so long. The storm caught me south of Fisher Lake. I had to dig in. I came on as soon as I could travel."

Skip was excited. "Buck found Blackie's body. Buck took shelter in a cave south of here and there it was. And he's sure now that a bear didn't drag it there!"

Jeff said quietly: "I'm sure of that, too. And there's something else I'm sure of. You didn't find the body of Blackie Barron."

It was right then that a cry of rage came from the clearing below. It was followed by a string of sulphuric oaths.

"Golly diamonds," Skip exclaimed, "what in the name of Moses have you got there?"

"What I've been trying to tell you is that that disappearing body you found in the cave is poor Willy Whiskers. That's Blackie down there caught fast in his own bear trap."

Buck Larrabee's jaw locked. He blinked. "Let's have that again. You've got *what* down there?"

"The killer," Jeff said. "Willy Whiskers's brother, Blackie Barron. And this time we have a live body for Jack Bailey."

20. The Reward

STATE TROOPER Jack Bailey was very pleased with himself and the world in general. His jacket was open and his feet were extended to the parlor stove. Crackling pine slabs sent forth an encircling warmth over the Hibbses' living room.

"I got the case all taped up," Jack assured the small gathering. "It's a very simple case, once you get the facts all sorted out and fitted into place."

Smiling dimly, Will Hibbs took his pipe from his mouth. "Once the boys captured the killer and presented you with the facts tied up in a blue ribbon, it was a lead-pipe cinch, eh Jack?"

"Don't look at me," Skip protested. "It was Jeff who figured it out. I think I'll turn in my detective badge and take up knitting."

Sitting on the floor with his back to the wall and his legs outstretched towards the fire, Jeff shook his dark head. "Don't give me too much credit. Holy ole mackinaw, I would have walked right into that trap if Hunter hadn't beaten me to it. Imagine that! I would have fallen for a curiosity set like I used on that wildcat. Blackie sensed someone was trailing him. He made a trail right over that grave, then left a red mitten there for curiosity bait."

"Blackie set that trap after Gaston figured out what was buried in that grave," Skip suggested. "I guess he figured he needed a little added protection when he was away from the camp and couldn't watch it from the window. I'm wondering how Gaston did figure it out. It's pretty clear that he did know but wasn't in any hurry to dig up the buried money. And it's clear that Blackie knew he knew and followed him back to his camp."

Will Hibbs took the pipe from his mouth. "We'll never know how Gaston learned the secret of the grave, but I've got a good hunch. Poor Gaston must have had quite a fright the night the wolf-dog answered his call. Up to that time he'd been trying to scare you boys with the wolf story. Then that day with Skip he saw those tracks." Will glanced over at Jack. "Could you tell the difference between a wolf track and the track of a large dog?"

"That part of my education has been sadly neglected," Jack admitted, "and I'm not unhappy about it."

"The fact is," Will continued, "most woodsmen agree that it's impossible to tell the difference between the track of a wolf and that of certain breeds of dogs. But tracks often reveal a lot more to a real woodsman than the mere register of a print. Ever notice how a fox, for instance, always circles and inspects an object from all angles before he finally ventures close? A dog, on the other hand, doesn't have the shy suspicious nature of his wild relatives. He'll approach something that interests him quite openly."

Skip had come forward. "That's right! The track came right up to the carcass and then went off again. That deer had been dead too long to interest Hunter. And once Gaston realized it was a dog that was running wild, the whole thing opened up. He knew it must be Willy's dog, for no house dog would be running that far in. If it was Willy's dog, then Willy must be dead, for Willy and Hunter were inseparable. If it wasn't Willy at Willy's camp, then it must be someone up to no good. And if Hunter wasn't buried in that grave — well, what was buried there? Sure, Gaston had known Blackie a long time. He must have known about that brother who had disappeared. All at once it all added up. Gosh, maybe I won't demand my money back from that correspondence school after all."

"You're doin' good, Inspector," Jack acknowledged with elaborate patience. "It must have been Blackie who called the sheriff to find out if his queer brother was still in this neck of the woods living like a hermit. Nobody knew what Willy looked like shaven. Only Blackie knew they looked enough alike to satisfy most anybody. Blackie had taken the alias of Dobson when he got out of jail. He got a job in a lumber camp and lifted that payroll. The police had such a good description of him and were hot on his trail that he knew he couldn't hide out for long."

"And when he hit that moose," Will couldn't resist adding, "his name was Quigley."

"That car he stole belonged to a guy named Quigley," Jack muttered. "This Quigley left his license in the glove compartment. Okay, so Blackie goes into the warden camp and grows some whiskers. Remember, he needed a shave bad that day on the road. He was already planning then to do Willy in and take his place. He hid out at the warden camp, waiting for his whiskers to thicken up a bit. When Buck and Jeff arrived, he decided you were just the ticket to find his body. The sooner the body was found with his identification paper on it, the sooner the case would be closed. He'd become harmless Willy Whiskers. Eventually he'd go back to civilization as Willy Barron and live like a king on that wad of dough. Neat, eh?"

Jeff shook his head. "Imagine laying a bear trap for your own brother! I guess that was the only way he could catch Willy. We should have figured that out when we saw that gnawed boot. I had that wolf on my mind and couldn't think of anything else, I guess. I still had the wolf on my mind when that body disappeared."

Will chuckled. "Jack laid it to a bear. Did you ever find the bear that moved that body, Jack? You could have that bear arrested."

"Maybe I was just kiddin' about thinking it was a bear," Jack defended. "Cops aren't as dumb as you think they are. Blackie knew that too. He wanted the body found and identified, but he didn't want the police to get hold of the corpus delicti. He didn't want to give us a chance to fingerprint that body. So he made like a bear and lugged it to that cave. It wouldn't matter if the body was found in the spring. There wouldn't even be any fingers left then. No sir, cops aren't so dumb."

"I've always said that, Jack," Will insisted innocently, "but I must say I've had quite a few arguments about it. I don't get any medals myself on this thing. I'm the guy who said Old Carrie's bump on the head had no connection with the case. Blackie must have been shadowing Willy that night he visited the warden camp. He overheard Buck shout after Willy that Carrie had sent him some kind of warning. He didn't know what Carrie suspected, but I guess he decided to take no chances. It's my personal opinion that Jeff and Skip are the ones to get citations in this case."

"We're not interested in citations," Skip said, "but I

told Jeff that at least he ought to have taken Hunter's hide in to Ernie Sampson and made him cough up that hundred bucks."

Jeff smiled. "I would have had Ernie on a spot. That Malemute breed certainly isn't very far from a wolf. I just figured that dog saved my life, and he was getting a decent burial in his own skin. Ernie hasn't graded our furs yet. We'll make out all right."

A car had stopped in front of the house. A moment later Warden Supervisor Bascom came stamping in with Buck Larrabee at his heels.

"Boys," announced Chuck heartily, "got some news for you. You don't happen to need a little pin money, do you?"

"You mean," Jeff asked, "Ernie Sampson has graded our furs? I didn't think there would be too much left over after he took out the stake."

The supervisor laughed. "Knowing Ernie, there won't be. The most valuable catch you made, Ernie wouldn't know what to do with. The insurance company that covered the stolen payroll, however, figured Blackie's worth about three thousand dollars, and you two trappers are going to get it."

The two boys sat dumb-struck. Ma Hibbs came out of the kitchen, drying her hands on her apron, and behind her came Pappy Newlin and old Gramp.

188

"Three thousand dollars!" Ma gasped.

"Three thousand dollars!" The two boys whistled in unison.

"A considerable bundle of lettuce," Pappy said judiciously.

"A bundle of little enough!" Gramp fumed, champing his gums. "Why you boys most got yerself kilt, didn't yer? Three thousand dollars! No wonder them insurance companies still got the first dollar they ever made!"

Jack Bailey slapped his hand against his knee. "I'd take that money without any fuss and put it right smack in the bank and stay clean away from the big woods the rest of your lives. What almost happened to you boys ought to teach you that the woods is a place for birds and animals. People ought to have more sense."

Will chuckled. "It'll take more than three thousand dollars to keep Jeff out of the woods, I'd like to wager."

"Boys," Ma interrupted, including the whole group in an expansive gesture. "You can spend that money for Jeff and Skipper after supper. I hope you all can eat. It's beans again."

"Beans!" Gramp snorted. "Beans again! I'm commencin' to look like a yeller-eye bean. Red meat is what a man needs to lard his ribs. Sunthin' he can get his chomper inter!"

None the less he was through the door one step ahead

189

of Pappy Newlin. The other men filed after them, following their noses toward the rich beckoning scent of Ma Hibbs's famous cooking.

Skip and Jeff loitered. Alone they faced one another, their eyes still incredulous.

"Partner," Skip exclaimed, "we've hit pay dirt! Do you realize how far three thousand dollars in one-dollar bills would go laid end to end?"

"I don't know about that," Jeff said resolutely, "but I can tell you where my share's going all in one pile. Will and Ma have often talked of building a set of sporting camps on the lake if they could ever lay some money by."

Skip thrust out his hand. "I'm in! What an idea! Why with our expert guiding and Ma's expert cooking and Gramp's expert lying, why we'll have the 'sports' coming from all over the country!"

"And be sure," Jeff warned, "you let Gramp do all the expert lying for the outfit."

Skip appeared injured. "Didn't I tell you I gave that up? That's gone with my youth. I discovered six hairs on my chin last night. Another couple of weeks at our winter camp, and I might have had whiskers like a regular old toe-pincher."

Moving slowly towards the kitchen, Jeff stopped. "Never mind the whiskers, partner. I've had enough of whiskers to last me the rest of my life!"

Skipper Doggett sighed in easy resignation. "My trapper's beard would have probably come out a dirty red. Let's go in and break the news. Loon Lake Sporting Camps. How's that for a name?"

"That sounds okay to me," Jeff agreed.

Together the boys headed for the kitchen.